THE SUITCASE MURDERER

a cruel killing shocks a small Yorkshire seaside town

JAMES ANDREW

Paperback published by The Book Folks

London, 2023

Second mass market paperback edition:

ISBN 978-1-80462-123-3

First edition published London, 2020

www.thebookfolks.com

To Pam and Ian

CHAPTER ONE

Birtleby was Inspector Stephen Blades' patch. Like any policeman, he knew what went wrong in it, and what went right; and it pleased him when things were quiet, as they had been lately. Like most towns in Britain, it was finding recovery from the Great War a slow process, but it was working on it. The men had returned and found their different ways to adjust to peace, though not all managed well. Women were adapting too. Some had lost men, and some had lost their chances of finding men; some had returned from wartime employment to domestic chores, and others were trying desperately to cling onto the greater independence that the war had offered them. Birtleby itself had found anew its pre-war cycle of rampant tourism in the summer, as the railway brought visitors to the town in what felt like hordes, followed by winters that were quiet, rainy, and windswept. Its small industries, too, were adjusting to peacetime needs. The button factory had returned to making buttons instead of military uniforms, and the boatyard was making fishing boats again.

There had been the usual cluster of drunken fights in the summer, petty vandalism, thefts, even an outbreak of a series of arson attacks in outbuildings – and the culprits had been found for most of these crimes. Blades knew that winter would be a less busy time. There would be domestics, from which they seldom achieved a result, as wives might make complaints but rarely stuck to them long enough for anything to reach court. Police constables and sergeants handed out well-meaning advice to them but with little hope. Drunken fights still occurred though there were less than in the summer, and there was the occasional theft if not as many; and the odd housebreaking.

The limits of what the police could achieve did at times depress Blades. Take the arsons. They didn't find out who started the fires, though local awareness had been built up to such a level that the culprit, whoever it was, had eventually taken fright and stopped. Blades pondered the purpose of the crimes. Had they been done by an adolescent with a misplaced grudge? Someone was giving expression to frustration, but serious harm did not seem to have been intended. In no case had there been danger to life, though things could have turned out otherwise, if any of the fires had gone out of control.

Blades often wondered at the emotions that lay under the bland expressions people presented as they went about their everyday business. As he walked down a street and glanced at them, he speculated about what those faces were hiding; he was aware everyone had secrets. He always noticed the instinctive nervousness people showed at meeting with policemen. Was it because of guilt at something they had done at some time, or at something they might be tempted to do, hopefully minor, though, as he knew, not always? At times, it felt as if he were walking amongst a series of unexploded mines. Who knew which detonator might be primed and ready? Yet, he reminded himself, these were ordinary people going about lives that would be for the most part reputable. It was his policeman's mind that saw the capacity for lawlessness wherever he looked, and he knew that, with most people, it would never come to pass. When it did, it often felt random, like those arson fires, but he knew there was a path that led to crime. He had heard it explained by countless criminals when they were finally brought to justice. Along the way, they had made choices, which might have appeared harmless but had culminated in a final decision that wasn't. They talked of the circumstances that had led to their misdemeanours, blamed their upbringings as often as not, and sometimes Blades could feel a measure of pity, though he knew these were excuses. Something had changed in them on their journeys. What had that been?

Blades tutted at himself, dismissed his musings, and returned to the task in hand. He was at his desk in the police station, studying a police constable's report. There was a gas lamp above his head, giving its patch of light. A conversion to electricity was scheduled but had not arrived. The report concerned a series of bicycle thefts. Constable Flockhart had caught the culprit in the act one night, and he had confessed to the others once he was under arrest in the police station. When Blades read the report, it initially read like an open-and-shut case, but he knew that depended on the presentation of evidence. Were the constable's reports accurately and properly done? Had the confession been taken under correct formal procedures? Blades shuffled the papers on his desk as he gave thought to this. Flockhart was off duty, but Blades would see him in the morning, with questions prepared.

It was quiet in the office. Blades was, for once, by himself. Sergeant Peacock had been at court that day, giving evidence in another case, and had not returned yet, though he would soon. The gas fire guttered. Wind blew rain against the window. As Blades glanced out, he became more aware of the darkness of the night, and the relative pleasantness of the office. Looking at the weather, it felt as if he was in an oasis of light and warmth.

Then the door opened, and Peacock was there, bringing in the brisk, late October air as he took off his heavy coat and his tweed cap.

'Did it go well?' Blades asked.

'We got the conviction,' Peacock replied. 'Not that we know the sentence yet.'

'It'll be a good one,' Blades said. 'Peabody's hard on burglary. How was defence counsel?'

'Leadbetter? As grim as usual. He tried to trip me up about the time of the incidents, but I was ready for him.'

'Good.'

'Any tea on the go? I could do with warming up a bit.' Peacock walked over to the stove and held both hands close to it.

The office door opened again, and this time it was the uniform of Sergeant Ryan that Blades was faced with as he stepped in with a report in his hand, and Blades wondered what it could be.

'What's the problem, Ryan?' he said.

'It's like this, sir.'

Sergeant Ryan was a large man with a firmly featured face that normally gave a reassuring impression of strength, so that when the lines of his forehead were creased into anxiety as now, it was disconcerting. Blades wondered whose psychological fuse had been lit.

CHAPTER TWO

Blades now found himself in the living-room-cum-kitchen of a worker's cottage opposite a worried-looking mother and father, and with Peacock beside him – still with no cup of tea but looking no less alert for that. The room was bare and simply furnished and Blades did not even give it a glance as he concentrated on the couple opposite him.

'You reported your daughter missing,' Blades was saying to Mrs Harkwright. 'Missing Person reports don't always involve me, but Sergeant Ryan expressed concern. So, when was the last time you heard from your daughter?'

'About a week ago,' Minnie Harkwright replied.

Minnie Harkwright was a middle-aged, broad-faced woman who looked a bit uncared-for, with untidy hair and a rumpled dress, as if more important things than her appearance concerned her. She had a kindly set to her face, Blades thought, but her most prominent feature was her anxious eyes.

'And you reported this when?'

'Yesterday.'

'Why so long in reporting it?'

'We don't see her every day. She's independent. She has her own place. It wasn't unusual to hear nothing from her.'

'You didn't worry at first?'

'No, but a week was longer than usual not to hear anything, and she is my daughter. I went over to where she's staying and got no reply. The whole place is locked up. Neighbours say the draper's shop hasn't been open in all that time and I've never heard of that before.'

'Has Emma worked with the Roots for long?'

'About a year. As an assistant. They give her a room above the shop too, staying with them, and she helps out in the house now and again. The Roots seemed alright to me. Perfectly respectable. You ask anyone.'

'I'm sure you look out for her.'

Blades agreed with her that Emma's disappearance sounded worrying. What made it of even more concern was that not only had Emma Simpson been reported missing, but, on inquiry, he'd discovered the Roots had disappeared too. 'Emma Simpson's your daughter's name?'

'That's right.'

'And you're Mrs Minnie Harkwright?'

'She married and then her husband died in the Great War, but she kept his name. I married again, too, if it comes to that. Andy died in the influenza epidemic at the end of the war. I was a Maitland then. But I found John, and we married and we're both happy Harkwrights now.' A fleeting smile found its way onto her face.

'I see.' Blades glanced across at her husband. John Harkwright was a short but burly man with large rough hands hewn in some working man's trade. He was bald with a thick moustache and sideburns, with a somewhat ill-favoured face, but strongly masculine, and Blades could see that some women would be drawn to him. He looked about ten years younger than Minnie.

'Do you think you'll be able to find her?' John asked, and Blades noticed a wheedling tone in his speech; John was at least giving the impression he wanted Emma found.

'We'll try, sir.' Blades allowed himself to study John Harkwright further. 'Were you here when Emma last visited?'

'Yes, he was,' Minnie replied quickly. 'And he's as anxious as I am.'

'I'm sure,' Blades replied.

Peacock lifted his eyes from his notebook at that point. 'Did you and Emma get on?' he asked.

'They did.'

As it was Minnie who replied instead of John, Peacock gave her a questioning look. 'Can't Mr Harkwright answer for himself?' he said.

Minnie didn't reply to that. John did this time, but he did not look towards Peacock but towards Blades. 'I've never been married before,' he said. 'Never had anything to do with children. I was ever so pleased Minnie said yes to me. And I wouldn't do anything to Emma.'

Blades registered the tone of indignation in John's voice as he spoke the last sentence.

'Did you find it difficult to adjust to becoming a stepfather?' Blades asked.

'I wouldn't say I was that,' John replied. 'Emma came along with Minnie, that's all, and she was fully grown, not to mention a widow herself.'

'She did come back to stay at first after her husband died,' Minnie said, 'but she's so independent. She was off like a shot when that situation at the draper's turned up. She was a draper's assistant before she married, so it was a place that suited her. But she'd have been welcome here. I know I had a new man about the house, but it wouldn't have worried me if she'd stayed till she found herself someone, though, mind you, how many men are there left to find after the war?'

Blades had watched Minnie carefully. Minnie meant what she said but Blades did wonder how convenient it would have been for them had Emma continued living with her and John; and he could see why Emma might not have wanted to be in the way and spoil her mother's chance of happiness. Or, were there other reasons why she wanted to be away from John Harkwright? Blades studied him again.

'What did you say you worked at, Mr Harkwright?'

'I didn't, but I work as a builder's labourer with Johnstone's, the local firm.'

'Have you been there long, sir?'

'Since I came back after the war. Mind you, I worked with them before I went out too, for about five years. It's a steady job. I'm lucky.'

'Quite. A lot of people struggled to get work again after the war. So, where did you serve?'

'I was out in Africa.'

'I expect it was difficult out there too, was it?'

'I'm glad I wasn't in the trenches. But yes, it was.'

Now Minnie entered the conversation again, an impatient look on her face. 'She was cheerful enough when she was last here – as ever. How could she disappear like this?'

'We'll do our best to find out,' Blades replied. 'What did Emma talk about the last time you saw her?'

'The usual things. What was it she was going on about then? Work. Customers who came in. The last row between the Roots.'

Peacock interjected again. 'The Roots don't get on with each other?' he asked.

'Emma says they do as long as Amelia does what she's told. And who can do that all the time?'

'I see,' Peacock said.

'Emma didn't mention she was seeing a boyfriend?' Blades asked.

'She doesn't have one at the moment.'

'There was one?'

'There was Alfred Duggan, but she finished with him.'

'Can you tell me more about him?'

'It was me that told her to end it with him.'

That sounded familiar, Blades thought. He came across that in his line of work, mothers warning daughters away from unsuitable men, and they could turn out to be worse than even the mothers thought.

'Which was why?'

'He was no good. He was a bigamist, and he did time for that.'

'Ah,' Blades said. Yes. Any mother would warn her daughter away from a man like that. He gave Mr Duggan some thought, then remembered he'd heard of him, when he'd come out of prison about a year before.

'When we found out about that, we told her all about him, and that was the end of that. Emma had enough sense to steer clear of the likes of him once she knew all about him.'

'Had she been keen on him?'

'Oh, he's a good-looking fellow and he's all charm. Women do fall for him. That's how he ended up in jail.'

'So, when did Emma split up with him?'

'Not that long ago, only a couple of weeks. But she had done with him.'

Blades gave that thought as well. When did parents know everything their children did or didn't do? No doubt Emma had said she would finish with her man to please her mother, but had she? 'Do you know how I might get in touch with this Alfred Duggan?' he asked.

'He works for Harrison's,' Minnie said. 'Though why they have any truck with him, I couldn't say. When he's in Birtleby, he stays in the Commercial.'

'We'll put some effort into investigating this,' Blades said. 'We will try to find Emma for you.'

'Thank you.'

And they had better check out the Roots' premises first, Blades thought. He stood up ready to go, and that seemed to be that, till Blades turned to face Harkwright. 'Incidentally, you still haven't answered Sergeant Peacock's question.' Blades hadn't liked the way Harkwright had skirted round the query. Harkwright looked shocked at attention being turned on him again.

'I'm sure I did. Didn't I? What was the question again?'

'How well did you get on with Emma, sir?' Peacock asked.

John looked flustered but answered quickly enough. 'I liked Emma. I always got on fine with her. Why do you ask me about that?'

Blades turned his glance to Minnie, who was looking indignant as well.

'John and Emma got on well. Just find Emma, will you.'

As he turned to go again, Blades simply nodded.

CHAPTER THREE

Blades and Peacock stood outside Roots the drapers with two constables beside them. It was a large Victorian building with spired roofing and weathered, dark stone, and there was something forbidding about it, perhaps the smallness of the stone-lintelled windows in the upper storeys, suggesting a lack of light inside.

On the ground floor, the shop itself had a large glass frontage with gold lettering in the sign above the window – *Roots: Draper and Milliner* – all calculated to draw the eye. But there was an eeriness about the window display of jackets and dresses, arranged as if for wear, but empty of the people they were made for. Blades wondered what they would find inside the building. He pulled the doorbell, which made a clanging sound deep inside the house, enough to waken the dead, Blades thought, then wished that hadn't occurred to him.

Blades waited for a few moments after the clanging had stopped as he listened for any sound there might be from inside, but there was nothing. Then he pulled at the doorbell again. The bell reverberated impressively but still provoked no response. Blades stepped back from the door and nodded to the larger of the two constables. Constable

Peters stepped forward, examined the door, then shoulder charged it but to no avail, although it shuddered. He stood back and looked at it again, then, lifting his right leg, he jumped at the door with his full weight behind his foot, which hit the door just at the handle. Fortunately, it was the door that gave with a satisfying snap. The constable tumbled in as the door opened in front of him, and Blades and Peacock strode in behind him.

Blades looked for an electricity switch but there wasn't one, so he took out his flashlight. They were at the bottom of a stairway. Blades flashed his light around, finding himself looking at walls and a shuttered window, before he started on his climb of the stairs. At the top of these was a hallway with several doors off it. Blades opened one, which led into a parlour. There was a gaslight. Peacock turned at the handle, then took out a match and lit the mantle. The gaslight sputtered into life as its pale glow spread through the room.

It was an ordinary front parlour with painted floorboards and rug runners, long sweeping curtains, velour-upholstered chairs and an ornate, carved, mahogany fireplace. Blades noticed that one of the rugs appeared to be kicked back out of place and walked over to look there. He held his flashlight and peered closely. There. Yes. Just there. On a floorboard, one or two dark specks of what looked like blood. He would have that confirmed. Blades peered round the rest of the room without seeing anything of note.

He and Peacock walked through the first floor, looking for signs of anything misplaced, something that might show there had been violent happenings here, in particular other signs of blood. Then they walked upstairs and examined the bedrooms and the bathroom. As Blades turned to go downstairs again, he thought at least they hadn't found a body. However, although there might be different explanations for the odd stain in the parlour, all of them innocent, no reason had yet been found for three people being missing from this house. Blades had just entered the parlour again and was looking around him, when he heard the shout. It was the voice of a man.

'What? Who did this?'

That was followed by a female voice.

'Someone's broken in. Don't go in, Thomas. They might still be there.'

But Blades noticed the advice did not deter Thomas as the sound of feet told. Then Thomas met one of his constables.

'Don't enter here, please, sir. This is a crime scene.'

'How dare you tell me what to do in my own house? I'll go wherever I like.'

Then Blades called out, 'It's all right, Constable, let them in.'

'As you will, sir,' the constable replied.

Blades found himself face to face with a red-faced, indignant-looking, large man in his fifties.

'Explain yourself,' Thomas Root said to Blades. 'What are you doing in my house?'

'Mr Thomas Root?' Blades asked.

'And who else would it be?' he replied.

'And this will be Amelia, your wife,' Blades said, looking at a slight woman with thin grey hair who had entered just after Thomas.

'Of course, it is,' Thomas said. 'And we live here. What are you doing in our house?'

Blades took out his card as he introduced himself. 'I'm Inspector Blades and this is Sergeant Peacock. There's nothing to alarm yourself with regarding your house, sir. We see no signs of a break-in or a burglary, though, in any case, you might like to check to see that nothing's missing. We're glad to see that you're not. That was a question which was raised with us. That's what we were checking up on – as is our duty as police officers.'

'Checking up? You've broken down my front door, which you'll pay for.'

'I'm sorry about that, sir, but you were not at home. Can you tell me where you were?'

'I was on a week's break at Amelia's sister's house in the country. Which is hardly out of the ordinary. Why would you think it was?'

Then something struck Thomas and he looked vaguely around him.

'Surely Emma told you that? She's here somewhere, isn't she?'

'Would you expect her to be?'

'Why yes. We left her in charge of the house and the shop while we were away. The shop had to be open as usual.'

'I realise this is difficult for you to adjust to, coming home to this. I'm sorry but it was necessary. We didn't know where you were, and we still don't know where Emma is – her parents have reported her missing.'

'What do you mean Emma's missing?'

'She hasn't been seen for a week.'

'But the shop. She must have been working in that?'

'It's been closed all week, which is why we thought something might have happened to her – and to you.'

'I see.' Now that Thomas understood the reason for police being in his house, he was calmer. Amelia was the more upset now.

'What can have happened to Emma? She's alright, isn't she?'

Blades searched for reassuring words but didn't find any. 'That's the question we're here to investigate. Do you know of any reason why Emma might have decided to go off somewhere?'

Thomas and Amelia looked at each other. Thomas's face took on a look of self-righteousness as he said, 'She had work to do. There was the shop to run, and the house to be looked after. What reason could she have had to go off?'

'Was there a young man she was interested in?'

Thomas gave a snort of what sounded like disgust.

'There was that Alfred Duggan,' Amelia said, 'for a while, but she finished with him.'

Blades noted the now familiar name.

'After what I caught her up to with him, she was definitely finished with him in this house,' Thomas said.

'Did she say she was planning to go away anywhere?'

'Not at all,' Thomas said, 'and certainly not when she was supposed to be working.'

'Did she have any friends we can talk to about her?'

'No one who came around,' Amelia said, 'and she didn't speak of anybody.'

'I see,' Blades said. A friendless young woman, he thought, and wondered if it was true. But he supposed he had found out what he could from the Roots for just now.

'Incidentally,' Blades said, and paused.

'Yes?' Thomas said.

'Is there any reason why there would be bloodstains in the parlour?'

'Bloodstains?' Thomas replied.

'In the parlour?' Amelia asked.

'Not that I know of,' Thomas said.

'That can't be true,' Amelia added, 'unless' – she paused – 'the maid did manage to knock over a bottle of port in there. It was newly opened too, almost full. I had to take that out of her wages, the careless girl. Would that be it?'

Blades gave that some thought. 'No,' he said.

'Then I can't think what that might have been,' Amelia said.

'I see,' Blades said, wondering about his, though he tried to keep the look on his face neutral. 'When would be the last time you saw Emma?' he asked.

Thomas looked across at Amelia. 'On the Saturday, when we were leaving, which must have been about… let's see… ten o'clock in the morning?'

Amelia nodded her head at this.

'How did you travel?'

'Why do you want to know that?' Thomas asked.

'It's just a detail. We like to build up pictures in our minds, that's all.'

'I see. We travelled by car,' Thomas replied.

'You said you were at your wife's sister's house in the country. Where exactly would that have been?'

'Ramshead.'

'I see. And how did Emma seem when you left?' Blades asked.

'Seem?' Thomas said, frowning as he thought about the question.

'Just as usual,' Amelia said. 'Nervous of the responsibility, I suppose, but I had the idea she was looking forward to it.'

'She didn't seem like anything, just as she always did,' Thomas said. 'She wasn't anxious or excited about anything. She could have done with worrying about things a bit more, I always thought. She had no thoughts in her head apart from what her romantic novels put there.'

Blades supposed that at least could be true.

'And could we just check with you which is Emma's room?' Blades asked. 'We need to check to see if she took clothes and baggage with her.'

'I'll show you,' Amelia said, and led Blades and Peacock upstairs to the top storey, where the three of them found themselves standing in a tiny room under the eaves, with barely enough room for all three to get inside at the same time. Blades and Peacock had already had a quick look round, but their eyes swept around the place with more care now.

It was a bare room with a narrow bed, a washstand, a wardrobe, and a chair, with not much room for anything else, apart from a tiny wall mirror and a religious tract saying 'Jesus Saves'. There was nothing cheerful in her room to keep her at the Roots', Blades thought.

'Her bag's still here,' Amelia said, pointing to the top of the wardrobe. 'She only had one, I'm sure, though I couldn't swear to that. Why would a girl her age own more than one case?' Amelia opened the wardrobe door and peered inside. 'There are a couple of spare dresses in here. I can't believe she didn't have more than that though I never paid that much attention to what she wore.' Then Amelia opened the wardrobe drawer. 'Plenty of underclothing here, which doesn't mean she didn't have any more. I don't know. I'm not being much help, am I?'

'Can you think of anything distinctive she might have been wearing?' Blades asked.

Amelia thought for a moment or two, then replied, 'She isn't a flamboyant dresser, but let's see. Oh, there was a ring she wore on her right hand – as well as the wedding ring on the left one.'

'Can you describe it?'

'Silver. With a heart shape, though she'd no initials on it or anything.'

'That could be useful,' Blades said.

'And she wore a bracelet. A silver one. A sort of chain. But I can't really describe it any better than that. Sorry.'

'Did she talk of going anywhere?' Blades asked.

'No. And she's never gone off before. I couldn't even tell you of anywhere she might have gone to.'

'I see. Thank you,' Blades said.

There being nowhere else to search in that small room, Blades and Peacock did not linger. If there was anything else they had thought they might be looking for, they had not found it.

CHAPTER FOUR

The Roots were displeased when they were told they could not stay in their own home due to their house and shop being a possible crime scene. Blades and Peacock needed time to search them properly. Fortunately, Thomas Root had a sister who also lived in Birtleby. The shop was searched this time, and the basement, as was an outdoor shed. As of yet, the only sign of anything untoward was the apparent bloodstain that Blades had spotted earlier.

Mr Root wanted to know when he could open for business again, but Blades could not tell him. With no signs of an incident elsewhere, he supposed anything that had occurred must have taken place in the parlour, and samples had been taken of the stain there. Meanwhile, Blades and Peacock busied themselves with fingerprint powder and photographs. Blades knew the necessity of being thorough, though he felt he could almost hear his Chief Constable's voice in his head. 'This is only a missing person case. Why are you spending so long on it? There's no body. You need one of those to prove it's murder.' But Blades knew he would not regret the time he was spending now if one did turn up. In any case, Blades had an ominous feeling. Bloodstains – and that is what he was assuming they were – in the most public room in the house, were worrying.

He ordered a meeting for the next day of the whole station staff so that he could delegate his sergeants and constables. The first thing to be checked was whether Emma had set off for somewhere. She had obviously left at short notice, anyway, if that was what she had done. If she had, someone must have seen her. Inquiries would be made at the railway station, and the tram and bus stations. Wires would be sent to different police stations within Yorkshire, and also further afield. Questions would also be asked at lodging houses, and hotels. If Emma was travelling, she needed to stay somewhere, though Blades wondered why she would travel anywhere, and apparently in secret. The most likely explanation might be because of a violent argument. Or, was she in debt? Was there a young man she was travelling with, or to – at the moment unknown to them?

They had little to go on, leaving only questions. Had Emma had an argument with Alfred Duggan? Was she afraid of him? They had been told by two different people that she had finished with him. Had she not succeeded in doing that? What had his reaction been? Or, leaving aside the unproven 'bloodstain', if her parents had forbidden her to have anything to do with him, could Emma and Alfred have run away together? If proof of violence at the Roots' premises did transpire, Blades would then order an extended search for a body in the local area, which was what he expected to end up doing. One thing they did need to do straight away was interview that Alfred Duggan, if he was still around.

CHAPTER FIVE

The Commercial was well known in Birtleby; it had been a popular lodging house with commercial travellers for the last fifty years. A plain-looking woman with greying hair, wearing a frayed home-knitted cardigan in dingy brown, greeted them as she answered the door. Blades gathered that the business, if well established, was not prosperous. The natural wariness on her face at the sight of Blades' card she dismissed with a shrug of the shoulders, as she showed them into the lounge with the wry remark, 'You've caught up with him then. And a good job too I'm sure.'

Blades and Peacock found themselves in a parlour. Blades was struck by the large maps in frames that decorated the walls. One was a map of Yorkshire, while another covered the whole of Great Britain, and, yet another, Europe, with business cards stuck higgledy-piggledy into the frames. Blades' impression was that these recommended other places where the fraternity of salesmen was welcome. The room was also filled with several, large-winged, worn leather chairs which were empty. In the furthest corner was a desk, with a phone on it, and various papers and writing implements; at this was seated a young man with a pen in his hand, writing in what appeared to be a book of accounts. This was Alfred Duggan.

'The police, Alfred,' the woman said, then laughed. 'What have you been up to now?'

Alfred put the pen down with a frown that was instantly dismissed in favour of a welcoming smile. Blades' first impression was that this was a man that women would be drawn to. He had a lean frame with broad shoulders, neat, fair hair that shone in the light, and unusual eyes; they were a light shade of blue that drew the eye, with a streak of brown in the cornea of each, and a luminosity that was compelling. Considering that Duggan was facing two policemen, Blades was impressed by the wholeheartedness of the look of welcome on his face.

'Sorry to disturb you, sir,' Blades said.

'No problem,' Duggan replied. 'How can I help?'

'I'll leave you to it,' the woman said. Blades thanked her as she left, then considered Duggan.

'I believe you know Emma Simpson.'

A hesitant look appeared on Duggan's face followed by one of decisiveness.

'I don't know who you mean,' he said.

Blades noticed that Peacock could not suppress a short laugh, and he resisted the temptation to do the same.

'You've been courting her,' Blades said. 'Her parents say so. They gave us your name and your address, and here you are, Mr Alfred Duggan himself.'

A vague look had overtaken Alfred's face, which was one that seemed prone to sudden changes.

'Emma?' Duggan said.

'She works at Roots, the drapers,' Blades said.

'A brunette,' Peacock said. 'Neat figure. Curly hair. Good legs.'

Duggan's eyes swivelled towards Peacock's. 'Ah,' he said, as he gave what appeared to be an impersonation of a man to whom something had dawned upon, which in itself turned into an imitation of a puzzled man.

'Emma? Wait a minute,' Duggan said. 'Yes. I did date someone of that name for a few weeks.'

'You've just remembered you dated her for a few weeks?' Peacock sneered.

'That's right. But I haven't seen her in some time. Is there a problem? Nothing's happened to her, has it?'

'That's what we would like to find out,' Blades said. 'She hasn't been seen for a while, which is why her parents have reported her missing. She was last seen about a week ago by her employers, the Roots, before they left for a week's break, leaving her in charge of the shop and house – not that she opened the shop all week. We wondered why. Can you shed any light on that?'

'I don't see how I can,' Alfred said. 'It's a few weeks since I saw her. We decided to stop seeing each other.'

'And what was the reason for that?'

'Sometimes things work out. Sometimes they don't.' He shrugged his shoulders. And now his face was one of bewildered innocence. 'Emma wanted to finish it. Maybe she'd found someone else. I don't know.'

'You wouldn't know who that someone else was?' Peacock asked.

'Or maybe she didn't. Emma wasn't all that specific about what the problem was.'

'It wasn't her parents, was it?' Blades asked. 'According to her mother, she'd warned Emma about you.'

'I suppose Emma did mention something of the sort.'

'You're a convicted bigamist and her mother had found that out?' Peacock said.

Alfred's expression was now one of controlled indignation. 'A spiteful thing to tell her, I thought, but predictable enough.'

'Especially as you're still married,' Peacock said.

'So, where's this going?' Alfred asked.

'Can I ask you again when the last time was that you saw Emma?' Blades asked.

Alfred pursed his brows in thought, and Blades did wonder why he would have to consider the answer quite so carefully.

'Three weeks ago,' he said. 'When Emma told me that she was finishing with me, following her mother's advice. We were in the park. It was raining. She walked out on me and told me to leave her alone. I did.'

'Which is two weeks before she disappeared?'

'That's correct.'

'We do tend to ask a lot of questions, and we ask them of a lot of people. If we discover you saw her later than that, it'll look suspicious.'

'Will it?' The expression on Duggan's face was now one of bland disinterest. Blades might have thought Duggan had been asked a question about the weather. Blades wondered what had made him apparently so less wary. And why the need for such defensiveness in the first place?

'Why did you deny knowing Emma Simpson when you so obviously do?' Peacock asked.

'You're the police. I knew something was up. I didn't know what it was.'

The bloodstain still preyed on Blades' mind, but he supposed none of this did necessarily mean Duggan had done anything to Emma. He had a record for liking women too much, not for violence. The man was probably just a habitual liar. That would fit with what Blades supposed of his lifestyle.

'We would like a statement from you about your relationship with Miss Emma Simpson and in particular the place and time of your last meeting with her.'

The look on Duggan's face was now indecipherable, but Blades noticed something had switched off that luminosity in the eyes.

CHAPTER SIX

There was a heavy silence while Peacock drove them away from the lodging house. As if replying to Peacock's thoughts, Blades said, 'It's women who fall for him, not men.'

Peacock gave Blades a questioning glance. 'You're right. I'm one man who didn't like the look of him,' he said. 'You wonder what women see in a man like that.'

'Some young women bend over backwards to convince themselves about a man when he's as good-looking as Alfred Duggan, and I daresay he has charm.'

'I can't say I come across that reaction from them,' Peacock said, with a look that suggested some misjustice might be afoot.

Blades laughed. 'You're the trustworthy sort. That's not what the kind of woman who falls for the Duggans of this world is attracted to. But the real question is: does he know anything about where Emma is, and did he have anything to do with her disappearance? He's ruthless with women. That's written all over him – but is he dangerous?'

'We can't rule it out.'

'No, but we can't rule out anything or anybody else either. When was the last time Emma was seen?'

'By the Roots on the day they left for their trip away.'

'So, she disappeared at the same time they did, which was the Saturday. Is that a bit much of a coincidence?'

'I don't like those.'

'So, there's a chance they were the cause of her disappearance?'

'Yes.'

'Stop the car here,' Blades said. 'We'll talk this through.'

They were on the seafront by then and Peacock pulled the car up at a spot overlooking the pier, which stretched its long sweep out into a wind-driven sea. Blades took out some Woodbines and offered one to Peacock. Pulling out a Vesta case, he struck a match and lit Peacock's cigarette then his own. Blades drew in a lungful of smoke and revelled in the acridness.

'There was something unconvincing about Mr Root,' Blades said. 'Why was he so slow in asking about Emma? When he found us in his house, the first thing he should have done is ask about her.'

'Drapers are odd people.'

'What makes you say that?'

'It's what everyone says. They have to pander to women all the time, find out their tastes and indulge them. And they have to dress themselves to suit their trade, in other words, above their class. A friend of mine was a draper's assistant once, not that he made the grade. He's much happier working as a mechanic, covered in engine oil all the time instead of hair oil.'

Blades laughed. 'The trade wouldn't suit everyone – but Mr Root himself is not an effeminate man.'

'That's probably why his shop isn't more successful. He doesn't fit the mould.'

'It's a small business,' Blades agreed.

'It's a surprise it survives alongside so many others in Birtleby. And the others are bigger and have a wider range of stock. That's what people say anyway.'

'We met him at an awkward moment, but he does look the bad-tempered sort. Alfred Duggan is all charm. The first thing you notice about him is his disarming smile, and the first thing that registers about Thomas Root is his frown. But is Root violent? And why would he do anything to Emma?'

Blades and Peacock sat looking out to sea. Peacock raised his cigarette to his lips.

'I wonder if he was tempted by her,' Blades said. 'Did he do anything to her? Rape her? And need to cover up afterwards? If there was blood all over the place, his wife must have known about what happened. I wonder if she would help him clear up.'

'She looked mouse-like to me. Would she be capable of that?'

'Would she be capable of disobeying her husband?' Blades asked.

Peacock thought about that. 'I wouldn't underestimate women who look meek,' he said. 'That look can hide a lot.'

'We need that blood in the parlour confirmed, and we need to know what else we can discover about it.' Yes, that was crucial, Blades thought, and there was a large part of him that hoped they would tell him it wasn't blood. 'And we need to examine that car of theirs.'

'It could even have been Mrs Root who killed Emma,' Peacock said. 'She could have found out about an affair between her husband and the girl and killed her in rage.'

Blades blew out some smoke and watched it drift away. 'Maybe,' he said. 'But with no body to examine, we don't have any way of telling whether it was done by a man or a woman.'

'Do you think there's any chance Emma's still alive?'

'That would be good, but after a week? Why hasn't she shown up somewhere? Why doesn't she get in touch? It's a lot more likely she isn't.'

'Where's the body?'

Peacock's question hung in the air. Blades looked out at
the waves but did not want to follow the obvious thought.
If the body was out there somewhere, they might never
find it. Hopefully, it wasn't. 'Where did the Roots go?' he
said. 'That would be somewhere to search.'

'And the whole of Birtleby,' Peacock said. 'If there's a
body, it could be anywhere around here. Where's the best
place to get rid of one in Birtleby?'

'Back gardens, back yards? Middens?'

'How easy is it to convict anyone without one?'
Peacock asked.

Blades gave Peacock a quizzical look. 'You haven't
heard of the "Campden Wonder" case?'

Peacock shook his head.

'It was a long time ago – in the 1660s. When a man
disappeared, they assumed he had been murdered, don't
ask me why because I don't know, but three men were
found guilty and hanged for it.'

'And?'

'There was only one problem. He wasn't dead. He
turned up two years later, saying he had been abducted.'

'Ah,' Peacock said. 'That was disastrous.'

'Hence the rule – no body, no murder.'

Blades took another draw from his cigarette and stared
out to sea, before turning back to Peacock. 'She might be
alive. We might find her. Inquiries are being made. We
need to continue with those. But we need to search the
Roots' place again too. If she's dead, there must be more
proof there somewhere. There's a lot of blood in a person.
There ought to be more traces somewhere, a lot more than
we've found so far. We could do with lifting everything,
carpets, linoleum, the lot. And they've a back garden, an
obvious place to bury a body, and it might have been
done. Though we'll need a court order before we could go
ahead with all of that.'

'Whoever did it has had a whole week,' Peacock said. 'They could even have cemented the basement floor over Emma.'

'Not the Roots, if they were away all that time, which we should establish. Where was it they went?'

'Ramshead.'

Blades drew in deep on his cigarette again before exhaling slowly. He looked across at Peacock and took in the frown on his face.

'I wasn't sure about those marks on that bath,' Peacock said.

Blades thought about this.

'The enamel's worn,' he said. 'They need to re-enamel or replace.'

'It was more than that, wasn't it?'

'In what way?' Blades asked.

'If you were cutting up a body in there, you'd want to make sure it wasn't obvious. You'd have some cloth, a tarpaulin, say, covering the bath before you started. But what if the saw cut through the oilcloth, not consistently but just when you couldn't avoid it. Would that fit in with any of those marks?'

Blades pondered this. 'We need to do a full search,' he said. 'Though, if her body's somewhere in the house, you'd expect to be able to smell it after this length of time.'

'That depends on when she was killed,' Peacock said.

'There must be traces of blood in that bathroom if a body was cut up there,' Blades said. 'They would have scrubbed away at that lino, but it's pretty worn. Some could have seeped through somewhere, the joins at least.'

Blades rolled down his window and threw his cigarette stub out. 'Loads of things to explore. Lots to do. We're only at the beginning of this investigation,' he said. 'Drive on, Sergeant. It's time we were back at the station.'

And he was thinking that the start of an inquiry was not a bad place to be. It was at least invigorating to follow different trains of thought through to see where they led, to work out scenarios; and what had happened did not need to be the worst imaginable. They could find Emma alive.

As Peacock drove the black police Model T Ford through the streets of Birtleby, Blades did his best to relax. He was pleased to have such a steady and skilful driver: Peacock's eyes were everywhere, anticipating any hazard well in advance. Blades was able to survey his beloved Birtleby in calm fashion: these cobbled streets and simple brick-built houses; these strolling men and women; these working carts; these rumbling horse-drawn carriages; these flashing cars; these buses; these trams; these bikes – all this bustle and this movement to and fro. Birtleby was so alive. That was why he revelled in it. And he knew what he wanted to do in this case: prove Emma was alive too, full of her laughter and youth and hopes and foibles. Blades had never met her, but he wanted to. And when they searched the Roots' place again, that would tell him surely which way this case was going to run.

CHAPTER SEVEN

The moment they arrived, a figure stepped out from under the blue lamp which announced 'Police' in unequivocal yellow letters above the shiny painted black door to the station. It was a tall man, who loomed in a way that seemed almost threatening. Blades recognized him straight away, John Musgrave, lead reporter with the *Birtleby Times*. There was no mistaking his fleshy face, or the broad felt hat and double-breasted overcoat, nor the perennial cheroot protruding from the thick-lipped mouth.

'So, what gives with the murder?' Musgrave said.

Blades considered how to respond to this, and decided it was as well to be open about the case. Coverage could be useful. It might bring forward someone who had sighted Emma Simpson. But his first reply was a question.

'What makes you think it's a murder?'

'It's what people are saying.'

'Who?'

'Neighbours. The word in the street.'

'They know better than I do. We have no body.'

'But Emma Simpson is missing?'

'Oh yes.'

'How do inquiries progress?'

Blades and Peacock glanced across at each other. 'You'd better go in and write up that report, Sergeant,' Blades said. Then he turned back to Musgrave. Something about the man's sardonic tone had put him on edge, but Blades did his best to ignore the reaction.

'Inquiries are at an initial stage. We have a lot of questions but no answers.'

'Were there definite signs in the house that there had been a struggle?'

'There were what looked like bloodstains, which are still being analysed. Even if it's blood, we don't know if it's human.'

'But the scene was suspicious?'

'When someone goes missing in mysterious circumstances, it always is.'

'What's the theory at the moment?'

Blades decided to ignore that question. 'We need to establish if anyone has seen Emma – in Birtleby, or elsewhere. It's possible Emma went somewhere else. We don't know why she would do that. Did she go with someone? If anyone has spotted her in the company of someone else – or by herself – it would be helpful.'

'Can you give a description?'

'Five foot four. Brunette, hair cut short. She dressed fashionably but we don't know what she might be wearing. She's slim, well proportioned. Twenty-three years old. She's from Birtleby, so speaks with a North Yorkshire accent. She's a war widow. She's been missing for about a week – since last Saturday.'

'The fifteenth?'

'Yes.'

'Is Alfred Duggan a suspect?'

How did Musgrave know about Duggan, Blades wondered. Musgrave had been digging.

'As we don't know if anything has happened to her, no one is suspected of anything.'

'But Alfred Duggan was hanging around her?'

'Alfred Duggan was seeing her, yes.'

'That's the bigamist, Alfred Duggan.'

Musgrave had worked out a story already, Blades thought, which was no surprise. He was a reporter with ambitions.

'That's the man,' Blades agreed.

'Could he have murdered her?'

'We don't know that she's dead.'

'She's been missing a week and she'd been seeing a convicted criminal. You're not suspicious he's done anything to her?'

'I might be suspicious of anyone who knew her, most of whom would be innocent.'

Now why, Blades wondered, was he protecting Duggan? The man had not come across well to him. Perhaps he was reacting to Musgrave. He was allowing that cynical attitude of the journalist to annoy him. He supposed it felt as if Musgrave was trying to be a caricature of a hard-bitten reporter.

'Is there any sign of a murder weapon?' Musgrave asked.

'As I keep on telling you, there's no sign of a body,' Blades replied, and an acid tone had crept into his voice. 'If anyone comes across one, could they let us know?' Then Blades laughed. That had sounded silly. 'No. Seriously,' he said. 'We don't know what's happened to Emma. One possibility is that she's dead. If she is, the murderer has the problem of disposing of the corpse. That's difficult. At least if Emma's body were found, we would know what happened to her. Obviously, we would prefer to find her alive, and the first line of inquiry assumes that she is. Has anyone seen her on public transport since the date of her disappearance? Has anyone seen her walking in the street? Has she taken up lodgings somewhere? Does a hotel owner or landlady recognize her from the description as someone who has recently taken up lodging with them? We need to try to locate her.'

'And if anyone had seen her with Alfred Duggan since she was supposed to have disappeared, that would help?'

'If she's been seen with anyone anywhere that will help.'

Musgrave had a fascination with Duggan, Blades noticed. This story was going to be slanted. He supposed it was Musgrave's journalistic taste for the lurid and sensational, and hoped the reporter's stories wouldn't lead the investigation. "Bigamist suspected of murdering young war widow" would make a good headline. He must try to make sure not to say anything that would corroborate that.

'Have you tracked down Alfred Duggan?' Musgrave asked.

'We've spoken with him, just as we'll speak with anyone who knew her. If any friends would come forward who've seen Emma in the last few weeks, we would like to talk with them, or with anyone who knew her even slightly and might be able to shed light on her feelings lately.'

'Is it true that Alfred Duggan's wife has decided to divorce him?'

Blades blinked. That was news to him. Why would Duggan's wife decide to do that now instead of when his bigamy came to light? But he would not be drawn into the world of Musgrave's reasoning.

'And when we have more information to give, we will announce it to the press,' he said as he turned to leave. The inside of a police station had never felt so welcoming.

CHAPTER EIGHT

It was Constables Flockhart and Rollins who had been trusted with door-to-door inquiries in Main Street where Roots the drapers was, and Sergeant Ryan was the person they reported to. They stood before him now in their contrasting shapes, the gangly Flockhart and the burly Rollins.

'A weary job was it, lads?' Ryan asked, surveying their tired expressions, as they appeared in front of him at the station desk.

'Tiring enough,' Rollins replied.

'And taxing enough,' Flockhart added.

'Let's hear it, then.'

Flockhart and Rollins duly extracted notebooks from their top pockets. Flockhart flicked his open, perused it, then looked up at Ryan as he started to speak. 'Directly opposite,' he said, 'live a pair of elderly sisters and you never saw such an odd pair. Thin as brush handles, with clothes even thinner.'

'Ethel and Anne Goodbody,' Rollins added. 'They've lived in that street for donkeys. Well past working age. You could hope they spend half their time peering out of the window at the Roots' opposite. But they don't, so they said, and they didn't see a thing. They did wonder why the shop wasn't open but weren't nosey about it, just got on with their own business. Pays you to mind that, they said.'

'So, if they did spot anything, they wouldn't tell us for fear of getting themselves into trouble?' Ryan asked.

'They probably spend half their lives glued to those windows,' Flockhart said. 'They spotted us before we knocked on their door. I saw those curtains move as we walked up to that place.'

'We'll bear that in mind,' Ryan said. 'If we need to, we'll question them again.'

'Then there were the Archers – next door to the Goodbodys,' Flockhart said. 'The husband is away so we should call back there. Mrs Archer has a high-handed way with her. I thought she was going to sort us out for not solving this already. Asked us almost as many questions as we asked her. And she says she did have a good look out from her window to try to spot what was going on when she saw that the shop was shut all week. But it was as quiet as a tomb, she said. Nobody going out and in. Didn't hear anything unusual.'

'On the other side of the Goodbodys,' Rollins said, 'are the Jennings. He's a teacher. At Birtleby High. He's another one who was out when we called, so we'll have to go back there too. His wife, Annie, was the garrulous sort. But she bent over backwards to be helpful. Talked non-stop about what a worrying thing it was.'

'And I don't suppose she saw a thing either,' Ryan asked.

'Nothing. Saw the Prudential Insurance man turning up at his usual time. Just after he called at the Jennings. Must have business with the Roots too. He knocked and knocked. Then he gave up and tramped off.'

'There was one thing that stood out,' Flockhart said, flicking through the pages of his notebook. 'Mrs Hannah Smith. Two doors down. Said the Roots didn't always see eye to eye. Amelia was a bit downtrodden. Thomas didn't give her much of a life. Always throwing his weight around.'

'Interesting,' Ryan replied. 'The more we know about the people involved, the better. Did anybody come up with anything else?'

Flockhart flipped back a couple of pages.

'Don't know whether to trust this one or not,' he said.

'Why not?'

'The last time Emma Simpson was seen was over a week ago?'

'That's right.'

'Harry Walker saw her on Wednesday. Clear as day and no doubt about it. Walking around the corner with a young man.'

'Did he give a description of him?'

'Tall, wearing a trilby hat. Couldn't tell the colour of his hair. Lean in build.'

'Is that as precise as he could get?'

'Yes.'

'Was he someone this Harry had seen around before?'

'He wasn't sure about that. He was sure of Emma Simpson.'

'Who's this Harry Walker?'

'A bit of a local character. Lives further up the street and across, and I've come across him before. One over the eight every night. You can hear him singing all the way up the street on his way home from the pub. We managed to catch him sober. Whether he was well lubricated when he saw or thought he saw our missing lady is the question.'

'So probably not a report to pay much attention to.'

Flockhart gave Ryan a doubtful look. 'He was convinced, though.'

'He went on and on about it,' Rollins agreed.

'So, it is a report to flag up to Inspector Blades?'

Flockhart and Rollins looked at each other.

'Maybe,' Flockhart said.

'Who knows?' Rollins said. 'He's a drunk. And for all we know he's trying to sound important and just making the whole thing up.'

'Which happens often enough,' Ryan said.

'Yes, but we probably shouldn't ignore it,' Rollins said.

'We won't. Anything else?'

'You'd think so,' Rollins said. 'Have you any idea how many people live in that street? We've about fifty reports between us. And others to follow up on who were out at the time. But no. The only one who saw anything was the dipso.'

'You'll enjoy writing that lot up though,' Ryan said. 'And there really was nothing else useful?'

'Everything much like the ones we've read out,' Flockhart said. 'Nobody suspicious hanging around. Nothing suspicious seen. Nothing suspicious heard. And when are we going to find out what's happened to Emma Simpson?'

'No one said they were particular friends with Emma?'

'No. And nothing illuminating in the picture they gave us of Emma. A self-respecting young woman who kept herself to herself. Not flighty. No gossip about visiting young men.'

'Not Alfred Duggan?'

'Oddly, no. He must have been discreet.'

'That would be his trademark from what I've heard about him.'

'There's just the matter of what this Harry Walker said.'

'A pity he didn't see her a couple of days earlier,' Ryan said. 'That would have tied in with what we know. We're not under the impression Emma was anywhere near there when Walker said he saw her; and it would be odd if she was still hanging around without opening the shop or giving any sign she was in there. Though you never know. The whole thing's a bit odd. Good job, though, you two. And you'd better get cracking with your reports. And make them good. Inspector Blades looks at everything carefully.'

Then Sergeant Ryan laughed. 'Keep you out of mischief anyway.'

CHAPTER NINE

Blades had been right in his conjecture about the angle Musgrave would take in his coverage of this missing person case. It was amazing how lurid the coverage of local crime had become in the *Birtleby Times* since Musgrave had arrived. It had been a tame and uncontroversial local paper before. The headline was much as Blades had worked out it would be. It read: BIGAMIST INVOLVED IN DISAPPEARANCE OF WAR WIDOW.

There was a full account of Alfred Duggan's criminal history, and a useful description of him plus a photograph, as well as the story of Emma's husband's war. Apparently, Luke Simpson had been a lance corporal who had been killed at Ypres. Blades had not known that. There was also an account of Emma's disappearance, and a photograph of Emma:

> *Emma Simpson was last seen on Saturday 15th October when Mr Thomas Root and Mrs Amelia Root left their home in Main Street to travel to Ramshead in order to stay with Mrs Root's sister for a week. Emma worked as an assistant in the Roots'*

store, the well-known drapers, also in Main Street. Emma was supposed to be looking after the house, where she also resided, and opening the shop while they were away but, not only was it closed for the entire week, Emma was not seen by anyone at all in that time. It was her mother, Mrs Minnie Harkwright, who reported her missing on Saturday morning as she thought it strange that she had not heard from her in all that time.

The police would like to know if anyone has seen Emma or knows where she is. She is not in the habit of travelling about. In particular, has anyone seen her in the company of any young man in that time? Emma is said to have stopped seeing a young man called Alfred Duggan a week or two before her disappearance. Does anyone know of anyone else she might have been seeing? Emma is described as being twenty-three years old, five foot four, with brown curly hair cut in a bob.

Does her disappearance have anything to do with Alfred Duggan? This is a line of inquiry that the police are following. Any sightings of her with him would be useful.

Blades sighed. Had he said anything specific about any line of inquiry at all, never mind one including Alfred Duggan? He supposed Musgrave would twist anything an inspector said to fit in with the story he wanted to write, which was irresponsible. This could turn into a witch hunt with Alfred Duggan the target – when they were still in the process of establishing the most basic of facts. Though, if any information did crop up that linked Duggan to this disappearance, that would be gold dust.

He turned from the newspaper article and started leafing through reports. Flockhart's account of Walker's statement drew the eye, and he studied it. At first sight, it looked spurious, but he wondered. He supposed there would be a few more sightings to evaluate now the article had appeared. If any corroborated what Walker said, that would be useful. Could Emma have been staying in that house during the first half of that week? Blades looked at all the reports on interviews with neighbours. No one else had described any signs of movement or given any suggestion someone was staying there. Could Emma have been there and been seeing Alfred Duggan? Even if Emma had attempted to make a break with him, with the Roots away for a week, Duggan would have seen their absence as an opportunity to try to have fun with her, wouldn't he? By Blades' reading of him, he wasn't the kind of man to miss that kind of opportunity. But why would Emma not be opening the shop? And why would she be keeping such a low profile in the house that no one in the street was aware of anyone staying there – apart from Walker? There was something there that did not make sense.

The phone rang on Blades' desk and he answered it. It was the proprietor of a small hotel in Hately, about fifty miles away, a Mr Faulkner. He was talking enthusiastically, and at length, about a young woman who had been staying in his hotel that week. He was sure that it must be Emma. She fitted the description exactly. She said she was there on a week's holiday. And there was a young man she had seen from time to time and he matched the details the paper gave of Duggan. Emma was a refined young lady and the young man was rough. Faulkner had felt sorry for her. Why did young women not see through the kind of men they attracted? He had tried to warn her against him, but she had laughed in his face. The rudeness of it. Imagine that. That was when he had decided she must be more brazen than he thought.

But, still, if anything had happened to her it was dreadful. Oh no. She wasn't at his hotel now. She'd left on the Saturday and no, she had given no forwarding address, which was a pity, and did any of that help? He would try to remember any more details if he could. Blades thanked him. After he had put the phone down again, Blades pondered. On the face of it, this was a good lead. It was even corroboration Emma had been seen with Alfred that week, as Walker had said, except it had not been anywhere near Birtleby, which contradicted the other half of Walker's statement. But there was nothing in Mr Faulkner's descriptions that could not have been gleaned from the newspaper coverage, and there could be similar couples around. For whatever reason, something told him this was not Emma, though someone would be sent out to question this witness further, and Blades would have further inquiries made in that area. There would be no end of helpful phone calls like these, and they had to be followed up on and recorded. Blades decided, with such a major case ongoing, it was time all incoming calls were dealt with initially by uniform.

CHAPTER TEN

When Duggan presented himself at Birtleby Police Station, this was to the surprise of Sergeant Ryan at the front desk, though Ryan did his best to hide it. He checked that Blades had the time to see Duggan, and ushered him into the office. Blades and Peacock looked up with a frank curiosity. Duggan was already a suspect, and they had not expected him to turn up of his own accord. Blades motioned Duggan to a seat in front of the desk, and Peacock pulled one up too.

'Good of you to drop in,' Blades said. 'How can I help?'

'I need to come clean,' Duggan said.

'You do?' Blades said.

The anxious look that had been written all over Duggan's face now turned to one of open innocence. 'It was on my conscience.'

Blades said nothing but waited to hear what Duggan had to say. Blades noticed that Peacock now had his notebook out and pencil in his hand, though Blades had not seen them being brought out.

'I lied.'

In the silence that followed, Blades listened to the office wall clock ticking and a car travelling over the cobbles outside, as he watched while Duggan's face went through a contrasting set of emotions, anxiety, relief, peace, then back to anxiety again. Still, Blades waited; he did not want to interrupt the process going on in Duggan's head.

'In the statement I gave, I said that the last time I saw Emma was three weeks before her disappearance was reported. I lied. It was just over a week before – on the Friday.'

'That would be the seventh?' Blades said.

Duggan thought for a moment. 'Yes. That would be about it.'

'Interesting,' Blades said. 'You made a statement and signed it.'

'It's complicated.' Then, after a pause, a rush of words came out of Duggan, completely unrelated to this. 'Did you find blood at the scene?' he said. 'You must have results from any tests that were made by now?'

Blades gave the question thought but did not reply.

'Who are you suspicious of?'

Again, Blades did not answer the query. He was not sure why he should be sharing progress with Duggan. Nor was he sure why Duggan's mind was jumping about in quite this way.

'So, you saw Emma on the Friday?' Blades asked.

'You must have some ideas?' Duggan asked.

There was a moment's silence before Blades spoke, and this time he did reply. 'We're making investigations but there's nothing we want to go public with,' Blades said, then repeated his own question. 'Did you see Emma on the Friday?'

Duggan's look in return was now a bit weary. 'Yes,' he said. 'As you said, the seventh.'

'When?'

'The evening. We went for a walk in the park. That was when Emma told me she was finishing with me.'

'And where were you on Saturday the fifteenth?'

'What does that have to do with it?'

Blades just gazed at him and waited again.

'Was that the day she disappeared?'

'Possibly,' Blades replied.

'I was travelling over from Dillingsworth. I have to travel all over with work, and it was time to come back here. But I didn't get here till the evening.'

'Do you have any witnesses?'

'Anyone who saw me I suppose, though I can't think of anyone in particular.'

'And you'll write a new statement explaining all this?'

'Yes. That's what I came in to do.' There was some truculence on Duggan's face but more resignation. 'You said if it came out that I'd lied it could go badly for me.'

'I did,' Blades agreed.

'I read the newspaper article. People will be coming forward saying all sorts.'

'And you'll be caught out in the lie?'

'Yes.'

'Have you more to tell us?'

'No.'

Having done what he had steeled himself to do, Duggan had a deflated look to him. He looked as if he was in a quandary about what he should say or do next.

'So, how did Emma seem? Had splitting up with you upset her?'

'It upset me. She seemed fine with it.'

'Did Emma give any hint she was going to go away anywhere?' Blades asked.

'No. She said the Roots were leaving her in charge while they went away. She didn't say anything about going anywhere herself.'

'Do you know where she might have gone?'

'No.'

'Was there anywhere she said she had visited before, and that she was fond of?'

'She didn't talk about that sort of thing.'

'Did she talk of other friends she had?'

'No.'

'She had no other women friends?'

'She didn't talk about them with me.'

They were getting nowhere, Blades thought. He noted the irritated expression on Peacock's face.

'Are you sure that was when she talked of splitting up with you?' Peacock asked. 'An empty house and Emma by herself would have been a good opportunity for a man with an eye to the main chance. You wouldn't try to take advantage of that?'

Duggan gave Peacock a wry look. 'It would have been a good opportunity. You're right. But I was out of luck.'

'And you just gave up?'

'Yes.' Duggan's look at Peacock had become icy. 'I don't force myself on women. She'd said no.'

'And you didn't take out your frustration on her in any way?' Peacock asked.

'I've no idea what you mean by that,' Duggan replied.

Now Blades took a hand again. 'Did you murder Emma Simpson?'

Duggan turned his eyes towards Blades and there was fury in them.

'No. Look, I've come forward voluntarily to correct my statement. Give me credit for that.'

Peacock was writing notes in his notebook. Blades was staring at Duggan. Duggan was now gazing at the floor; he was struggling with emotions that weren't feigned, and Blades tried to analyse them. Then Duggan turned his eyes back to him.

'I didn't. No.' And his tone was firm and clear. 'So, you haven't been getting anywhere with your inquiries? You need someone to pin this on?'

Blades looked back at him steadily. 'We're making progress, sir.'

Another silence fell, while Blades again waited.

'Has anyone turned up saying they saw me with Emma?' Duggan asked.

'When?'

'Whenever. You tell me. You're the one who's leading the inquiries.'

'When would they have seen you with her?'

'Not after the Friday night I told you about.' There was a firmness in the way Duggan said that.

Then Duggan was the one asking the questions again, which Blades hoped would give Duggan the chance to trip himself up.

'No one's mentioned anyone else she might have been seeing?' Duggan asked.

Interesting, Blades thought, but did not answer.

'You know about Russell Parkes?' Duggan continued.

That was a name new to Blades and he did reply to that. 'No. Who's he?'

'He's someone Emma saw from time to time,' Duggan said.

'Did she?'

'Yes.'

'So, tell me about him.'

'I warned her against him. But that doesn't mean she would listen. He lives in Birtleby. He's single, and he lives with his parents. Age? I don't know. About mid-twenties?'

Blades was intrigued. 'So, what's wrong with him?'

'Nothing on the surface. But he hates me, and Emma had been seeing me, so she had to watch out for him.'

'Why does he hate you?'

'He thinks I got him turfed out of his job.'

Blades found that interesting. 'And did you?'

'He works for the Prudential now. I knew him when he was working at Leighton Insurance. He was short with his takings one week and I helped him out.'

'How could he be short like that?'

'He'd been dipping into the pot.'

'So, you helped him out? How?'

'We know each other. Salesmen often do. He was talking about it and I lent him money to get him out of the jam – which he didn't pay me back. But his bosses still caught up with him about his accountancy habits. He must have dipped into the till before. He was convinced I must have tipped them a wink. Not that I did. But he's had it in for me ever since.'

'And you think he might have taken this out on Emma?'

'How would I know?'

'So, why are you telling us this?'

'You're making inquiries. If any witnesses come forward saying they've seen Emma with him–'

'We now know something about him. We do. Thank you for that.'

Blades drummed his fingers as he gave this some thought. None of the reports had mentioned anyone called Russell Parkes.

'What does he look like?' he asked Duggan.

'About the same height as me. But he's got black hair. Thin in build. A bit weedy, to be honest. Oh, and he has a gold tooth. Top right.'

'That sounds a useful thing to know.'

Blades thought of the variety of witness sightings of Emma that had come in. He was hoping some of them were true, because it would mean she was still alive – and there was one that fitted in with the description Duggan had just given.

'Thank you for your help, Mr Duggan. It's appreciated, and, as you've changed your statement, that does mean you'll have to make a new one.'

'I suppose,' Duggan replied.

'If you go with Sergeant Peacock now,' Blades said, 'he'll take it from you.'

Then Peacock led Duggan through to an interview room.

Blades considered Duggan. He had turned up at the station because he wanted to know where the police were with their investigations, and Blades wondered why. He also wondered if Duggan was trying to lead them in a different direction, one away from himself. Why would he do that?

CHAPTER ELEVEN

When the results of the test came through, Blades was pleased. Not only was it definitely blood, and mammalian, it was human, which justified the necessary court order.

He, Peacock and numerous constables stripped the Root premises bare. Every floor covering was raised; every floorboard was searched under; walls were tapped for potential hollows; the backs of cupboards were stripped out. The Roots would no doubt be devastated but a woman had gone missing and had probably been murdered. Nothing was gained from most of the destruction they unleashed, but they did strike gold in the bathroom. Peacock's instincts about the marks on the bath looked to be justified. When the lino on the floor round the bath was raised, more signs of blood were found; there were signs there had been a big blood spillage there, and samples were taken of that blood too. After that, the bath was dismantled, and taken away for further examination. The exact nature of those odd scratch marks would be verified. Piping was uncovered and taken out too.

When the bath drainage was examined, pieces of flesh were found there – and blood in the U-bend. Blood had flowed out of this bath, and, most likely, a lot of it. This was more to be sent for analysis. But it was already obvious, things were much as Blades and Peacock had dreaded. A body had been sawn up in that bath. Disposal of a body was a problem, as Blades knew well. Murder wasn't difficult to commit, or a person could be killed accidentally, but if someone wanted to cover up afterwards, there was the massive problem of what was to be done with the corpse. This one had been cut up and disposed of in pieces. It was a gruesome and distasteful find, but this was progress. Blades moaned. Peacock tutted. Neither took pleasure in the ground they'd just gained in their investigation, but it did simplify things. They could stop trying to find out where Emma might have travelled to because she hadn't gone anywhere. Those reports of sightings were so much fiction or wishful thinking, attention-seeking, self-glorifying fantasy, avenues that had to be considered at the time, but which could now be dismissed.

Blades shook his head with the thought of the police time wasted over misleading witness reports. It had felt like wading through mud at the time. At least one avenue of investigation had led somewhere, if exactly where he had not wanted. Blades thought of what he had discovered about Emma so far, her resilience and her independence, and he thought what a dreadful waste it was that she had been reduced to a few scraps of flesh in the drainage of a bath, and a few drops of blood. But this would give direction to the investigations. Circumstances supposed these were the remains of Emma Simpson, and Blades and Peacock were convinced, though Blades realised this might not be held as conclusive proof in a court. If they could find the rest of this body, that might be. But Blades knew that, in attempting to be deceptive, murderers could succeed. If the police did find the rest of Emma, could it be definitely proved, even then, that it was her? Nevertheless, the search would be made. It would involve a lot more man-hours but now they would be easier to justify to Chief Constable Moffat.

Had it been the Roots who had killed her, or Alfred Duggan – or this mysterious Russell Parkes that Alfred Duggan had suggested? If the Roots had been involved, that gave a wide search area. The body could have been disposed of en route to Amelia Root's sister at Ramshead. That was fifty miles away. They could not possibly cover every inch of that. They would have to look at maps and work out possibilities. Local police knowledge would help. Closer to home, Birtleby would have to be subject to a thorough search. Every back yard and garden, every shed, would have to be looked through. Left luggage lockers too. Beaches would have to be patrolled in case the body had been disposed of at sea and was washed in. And there was always the possibility the body had been packaged and sent somewhere else. That had been done before. Railway transport police would have to be involved. And there was something new to ask the public for help with. Had anyone seen anyone carrying anything suspicious? Or disposing of anything odd?

And who had done this and why? If the body was found, they had to hope that would provide a trail that would help. Blades thought of Duggan. The man looked slippery, but why kill Emma? Emma could do him no damage. Or could she? Had she found out about Duggan's wife and threatened to tell her? Who knew what dynamic that might result in? The Roots still had to be considered. Every effort had been put into hiding the fact a crime had been committed on their property, which might suggest they were involved. If it was Duggan, why would he take such care over that? To disguise the fact a murder had been committed at all? Perhaps he thought if a body wasn't found, there was no proof of murder and no one could be convicted. Perhaps he might even be right. Blades was pretty sure it was likely to be either the Roots or Duggan, but he supposed he should find out something about this Russell Parkes. Blades knew that in most murder cases the most obvious suspect turned out to be the murderer. But there was no guarantee this one would follow the pattern.

CHAPTER TWELVE

Blades did not remember Musgrave being as pushy as this during previous cases. He and Peacock had only just stepped outside the Root premises when they met up with him. It did make Blades rack his brains. Was there something he wanted to tell Musgrave at this stage or not?

'Is there a body?' was the question Musgrave asked. Straight to the nub of the matter. Still, it was simple enough to answer that one.

'No,' Blades replied.

'You're really ripping that place apart now,' Musgrave said. 'What's the lead you're following?'

'No lead. Due process,' Blades said.

'You wouldn't get the warrant for all that without something. What's up?'

'When we're ready to release a statement, you'll be the first to know,' Blades said, though he did wonder if he should just make one now. The sooner the public was aware there was a body to be found, the sooner someone might come forward with useful information.

'Is it true Emma Simpson was seeing another man, Russell Parkes?'

That surprised Blades. Where was Musgrave getting his information from? Blades had not known Musgrave to be this sharp before.

'And he's another shady character, isn't he? Wasn't he dismissed from his job with Leighton Insurance for embezzling?'

'Where did you get that information from?' Blades asked.

'It's public knowledge,' Musgrave replied.

'Maybe,' Blades said, 'but how did you come across it?'

'Asking around,' Musgrave said.

He had been a busy beaver, Blades thought. And he was doing well. Had he ever considered joining the police force?

'Are you saying that there's a reason to suspect Russell Parkes of being responsible for Emma's disappearance?' Blades asked.

'He was seeing her.'

Corroboration of that apparently, Blades thought. 'Who told you this?' Blades said.

'I've been interviewing neighbours,' Musgrave said.

The same neighbours who didn't tell us a thing about Russell Parkes, Blades thought. What kind of silver tongue did Musgrave have to persuade people to talk to him? Perhaps they were just wary of talking to the police.

'When was he seeing her?' Blades asked.

'The week before she disappeared,' Musgrave answered. 'They were seen walking about the seafront together, and he called at the house.'

'Nobody told you about his calling on the day of Emma's disappearance, did they?'

'Saturday the fifteenth? Unfortunately not. That might have been telling.'

'Can you give me the names of your witnesses?' This had to be followed up.

'You know I can't reveal the names of my sources. Nobody would talk to me otherwise.'

'This is a murder inquiry. Do you want to be charged with impeding the investigation?'

'No, but I still can't divulge sources.'

Drat, Blades thought. That whole street would have to be interviewed again. Well, he wasn't giving the responsibility to constables this time. Perhaps he could do some of this himself, or use sergeants, even one of the other inspectors.

'What can you tell me about Russell Parkes?'

'Apart from the fact he works for the Prudential?'

Something else Musgrave was up to scratch with, Blades noticed. 'Yes.'

'I can tell you where he lives. I don't want to be totally unhelpful.'

'That would be useful,' Blades said with a due note of gratitude, though he was still smouldering inside. Musgrave gave the address.

'You say he was dismissed for embezzlement?' Blades said. 'Was he charged?'

Blades did not remember such a case going through Birtleby Court or Birtleby Police Station.

'It was swept under the carpet,' Musgrave replied. 'Apparently, he agreed to leave. I don't suppose they wanted to dilute public confidence in the company.'

Blades tried Musgrave again. 'You wouldn't tell me who told you that?'

Musgrave grinned, but did not reply. Blades did his best to make his expression as inscrutable as he could. It was good to have a lead confirmed, but it would have to be followed up, and there already was so much that needed to be done. He needed to interview Amelia Root's sister and husband and find out if there was anything dubious about the Roots' week away; and there was the search for the body to be organized. It had been a trying day. He did not often come across such conclusive evidence of foul play; and having to give up hope on finding Emma alive had hurt. But perhaps this meeting with Musgrave could be turned to good purpose. He did now have ideas for a press statement.

'It would be helpful to release information to the public,' he said to Musgrave.

'Yes?' he replied, and Musgrave's face had lit up.

'A further search of the Root premises has led us to the unavoidable conclusion that there has been foul play in that house. We now do not expect to find Emma Simpson alive. The co-operation of the public is requested in the search for Emma's body. Has anyone come across signs of a newly dug grave in nearby woodland, or is there a bag lying somewhere which is attracting flies, or which smells horribly? Has anyone seen someone carrying anything from the Root premises? Has anyone been seen anywhere carrying a suspicious package, one possibly bloodstained, but which would be too large to contain meat from the butcher's? The police will be conducting a thorough search of all nearby areas where a body might be expected to be discarded or hidden. We may not have found Emma but, if we can find her body, then that may lead us to her killer.' Blades stopped. He had probably said as much as would be helpful now.

Musgrave was still writing it all down as Blades turned away. There was a lot to be done, and he must make sure Musgrave did not take charge of the investigation.

CHAPTER THIRTEEN

It was Sergeant Ryan who came across the vital witness. Door-to-door inquiries had begun in Main Street again and Ryan was interviewing a nervous-looking young woman who lived several doors down from the Roots' and on the same side of the road. Someone in that position might not be expected to have spotted very much so Ryan had not been hopeful, but he knew as well as anybody it was often the last person you might expect who had seen something.

Agnes Braithwaite was a war widow with one child, which probably explained her anxious look. In all likelihood, it never disappeared. Ryan noticed that she had a pinched sort of face as if she did not get enough to eat.

'I don't want to get into any trouble,' she said. 'I didn't think it was important. I would have mentioned it to that constable who came around, but I didn't want to waste his time. People must tell you all sorts of things, busybodies that they are. That Alice Roberts down the street, I bet she had a tale to tell. Talks non-stop that one, and about nothing usually. If she hadn't seen anything, she would make something up to look important. I wouldn't do anything like that.'

'So, you did see something?' Sergeant Ryan said.

'That's what I'm telling you, isn't it?'

'Only you didn't think you had at the time.'

Agnes' face brightened.

'That's it,' she said. 'You've hit the nail on the head. The minute that constable left, I thought – now should I have told him about that? And I worried myself sick about it, but I was sure he would say it was nothing. And he looked so busy. And you must have a lot to do when you're doing this sort of investigation–'

Sergeant Ryan could wait patiently no longer.

'What did you see?'

'It's like this…' Agnes paused while she collected her thoughts. 'I mean, it's nothing. People go walking about with suitcases all the time, don't they?' Then she stopped again and looked at her feet, and Sergeant Ryan could sense she was starting to feel foolish.

'You're right. They do. So, something must have caught your attention about this person.'

'He had this furtive look. He'd just come out of a door further up the street. I could swear it was the door to the Roots' house only I didn't actually see him coming out, did I?'

'And what was odd about this man?'

'He had such difficulty lugging his case about. He had to put it down and give his arm a rest, then pick it up with the other arm. And he looked strange. Sort of white as if he was scared. When he looked up and saw me, he gave me ever such a glare.'

'You had a good look at him then?'

'He was scaring me. I daren't look at him when he stared at me like that. I just looked anywhere but at him.'

'Can you tell me more about the suitcase?'

'It was a big one. Brown leather. Sort of worn and old-looking with travel stickers on it.'

'Did you see what the stickers were?'

Agnes thought carefully. 'No,' she said.

'Would you recognize him again?'

'I don't know. Maybe.'

'What did he look like?'

'Tall, I suppose.'

'Colour of hair?'

'He had a hat on. I couldn't tell whether he was blonde, dark-haired or what. He had a thin sort of face and glaring eyes like I said.'

'Looked a bit like a murderer, you mean?' Ryan could not prevent the remark. A man with glaring eyes sounded fanciful.

'What do you mean? Here, all right. You ask someone else then. I know what I'm trying to tell you. If it isn't any good, it isn't. Fair enough.'

'All right,' Ryan said. 'All right.'

'Well, he would have glaring eyes if he was glaring at me, wouldn't he?'

'I suppose,' Ryan said, now beginning to feel a bit foolish himself.

'He gave me a right evil look. That was what made me feel I might have caught him doing something he shouldn't have. Which was why I thought I maybe should have mentioned it. But you're right. It doesn't seem that much. And now I feel I shouldn't have said anything at all. I don't know. Did I do the right thing bringing this up? I'm sorry if I didn't.'

'Oh, you did the right thing,' Sergeant Ryan said. 'Believe me, you did. And when was it you saw him?'

'Must have been the Monday.'

'The seventeenth?'

'That would be it. In the middle of the afternoon some time. About three at a guess.'

'Is there anything else you can tell me about what he looked like?'

'I don't know. I'll have to think. Quite tall, like I said, quite lean. A slouch hat on, so I couldn't see his hair. Apart from that, I don't know. He didn't look out of the ordinary at all.'

'He didn't?' Ryan asked.

'Just his eyes. Like I said. They scared me. I looked away and tried to pretend I hadn't seen him.'

He had the eyes of a murderer I suppose, Ryan thought, back to wondering just how much of this was fantasy and how much wasn't. But it would be written down faithfully, and Inspector Blades would make of it what he wanted.

CHAPTER FOURTEEN

The Southwicks' house was a large, stone-built property with a columned portico and tall Georgian sash windows. It was in set in a well-to-do area of Ramshead amongst others of the same ilk. Blades and Peacock looked at it with bemusement. So, this was the bolthole that the Roots had disappeared to when they left Birtleby? Blades supposed it would be a shock to Amelia's sister and her husband if the police had to treat this upmarket property in the cavalier manner they had the Roots' place. Blades announced their arrival at the front door, where he handed over his card. After it had been taken somewhere into the depths of the building, and presumably inspected, they were shown in.

They found themselves in a drawing room with silk drapes and a high, plaster-corniced ceiling, where Mr and Mrs Southwick awaited them.

'I trust this will not take long' was the welcome that was barked in Blades' direction from a bald, bespectacled, tall, and somewhat over-dignified-looking gentleman somewhere in his mid-fifties. There was a redness to his complexion that suggested a fondness for port or some other beverage of the type, and a stoutness that did not belie this.

Blades made his expression as neutral as possible in return. 'Hopefully not,' he replied, 'but there are questions we need to ask, if you don't mind.'

If you don't mind? Blades thought. This was a murder investigation. It did not matter whether the self-important Mr Southwick minded or not, but Blades was also aware this was a solicitor he was dealing with, and that it would do no good to attempt to ride roughshod over him. Southwick's knowledge of law was definitely greater than that of a policeman.

'I can vouch for Thomas Root,' Southwick continued. 'A most estimable man with a reputable business.'

Blades noted that Southwick knew why the police had arrived at his doorstep without having to be told.

'Thomas always makes sure he's on the right side of the law,' said the lady to Southwick's right. Blades wondered if she realised that made it sound as if the good Thomas skated round it. 'He's always been considered most respectable.'

Blades tried to take in the woman. This was Helen Southwick, Amelia's sister. His initial impression was that downtrodden women seemed to run in the family, though, physically, there was a marked difference between the sisters. Helen Southwick was about the same height as Amelia, but with no other resemblance that Blades could see. This woman was stout and particularly homely, with long hair tied back in a bun. This was not a robust stoutness though; there was a faded look to those eyes, and a subservience in the glance she gave her husband.

'As no doubt are you,' Blades replied.

'Quite,' Southwick said.

'It's unfortunate that inquiries led us to his door – and, subsequently, to yours.'

Blades let those words hang in the air; he had been courteous but there was a job to be done.

'So, how can I help you, Inspector?' Southwick asked. There was a compliance in his eyes, but Blades sensed that it was reluctant.

'As I'm sure you are aware, we are investigating the disappearance of Miss Emma Simpson, a young woman in the employment of Thomas Root of Birtleby.'

'I am,' Southwick replied.

'You may not know all the circumstances of that disappearance, but the last time that Emma was seen alive was on the morning of Saturday the fifteenth, and the last people to see her were Mr Root and his wife Amelia. Your sister,' Blades added with a nod to Helen Southwick. 'That was the day that they came over to stay with you?'

'Yes,' Southwick replied. 'They motored over and arrived – I don't know – late afternoon some time.'

'You couldn't say when exactly?' Peacock asked.

Southwick gave him a look that suggested he was surprised that Peacock was entering into the conversation.

'They arrived at about five,' Helen said with a quickness that Blades wondered about. Was Helen wary of her husband's replies?

'Before or after five?' Peacock asked.

'Just after,' Southwick said with a brusqueness that invited no further questions.

Peacock wrote down the reply.

Just after five? Blades was thinking. They knew the Roots had left just after ten. It did not take that long to motor fifty miles, even on those country roads, and he wondered what the Roots had been doing in the meantime. Blades did not suppose the imposing solicitor in front of him would allow his position to be jeopardised by involvement in the disposal of a body. If the Roots were guilty, they had divested themselves of their corpse on the way.

'How did they seem when they arrived?' Blades asked.

'Much as usual,' Southwick replied. 'When they are coming here to stay, that is. I think Thomas gets a bit weary in that shop. I suppose anyone would. I know what dealing with the public is like. I do in my job. And I should think it's much worse in his. Customers can be a demanding lot. I suppose I am too when I'm out and about. Money doesn't come easily for anyone, so I like to get value for it.'

Blades wondered if Southwick was talking to give himself time to think.

'But to return to your question. How did they seem?'

Blades could see the lawyer's mind working at the exactness of the words he used.

'As I said, he was tired. But he was cheerful. He was in a good mood and looking forward to his stay.'

'So was Amelia,' Helen said. 'Chatting nineteen to the dozen about the latest clothes that had come into the shop and how I should dress up a bit more. She is like that. Always looking out for you and making suggestions. And she was ever so pleased to get away. Birtleby's such a boring place, according to her. And she likes the street we live on. She says it's ever so fashionable.'

'Nothing suspicious there, then,' Blades said. 'And nobody was sporting any bruises or anything of that sort?'

'Certainly not,' Helen said.

'No,' Southwick replied.

'And they stayed all week?' Peacock asked. 'They didn't go away at any time?'

'We did the social round,' Helen said. 'I took them out and about. And we did some walking on the moors out at Falcombe. Helen likes to get fresh air. Proper country air, she calls it.'

Falcombe? Blades thought. He supposed that would be a good place to dispose of body parts, though he did not see Helen helping with that.

'Whereabouts at Falcombe?' Blades asked.

'I don't see why it matters,' Southwick said.

'If it doesn't matter,' Blades said, 'there's no reason not to say.'

'On the path towards Highcombe, then back along the same track,' Helen said.

Blades nodded. He could visualise where that was. And it would be searched. There would be a lot of searching. Fifty miles between Birtleby and Ramshead, and body parts could have been disposed of anywhere on that route. There would be much poring over of maps to decide areas of interest. Moffat would hate all this expense.

'Did they ever talk about Emma with you?' Blades asked.

'Not a lot,' Southwick said. 'They did mention her. Said they thought they had a steady employee there. If they could keep her away from men.'

'Did she gad about a lot with them?' Blades asked.

'I don't think it was that,' Helen said. 'There was one unsuitable type they mentioned. Not a stream of them, no. My sister's husband wouldn't have put up with that.'

'Did this "type" have a name?' Peacock asked.

'They didn't mention it,' Southwick said.

'They didn't talk about Emma much,' Helen said.

'She was staff. They made a passing comment. That was all.'

'You're sure they only mentioned one man?' Blades said. 'There wasn't someone else as well?'

Southwick and Helen looked at each other. Helen looked a bit bewildered by this.

'No,' Southwick said. 'They didn't mention anyone else.'

'I don't suppose you know the names of any of Emma's other friends, do you?' Blades asked.

'No. We don't,' Southwick replied.

And that was that. Blades was not under the impression this pair had been involved at all. Nor did they know anything helpful.

'I'll have to ask you to make a statement,' Blades said. 'I'll make an appointment for you at your local police station.'

'Statement?' Southwick asked. 'But why on earth? Surely, you don't seriously suspect Thomas of anything?'

'It's a murder inquiry, sir. It generates a lot of paperwork. And it's the best way to eliminate people from inquiries.'

Southwick gave Blades a malignant stare, which Blades found uncomfortable.

'The best way for you to help your brother-in-law is to help us get facts straight. I'm sure you're right and he's in the clear. And the best thing you can do to help him is give a detailed statement.'

Not that Blades had dismissed the respectable Mr Thomas Root from his inquiries or would after reading Mr Southwick's statement. He had more questions to ask Mr Root.

CHAPTER FIFTEEN

Chief Constable Moffat had summoned Blades, and the inspector now sat on a hard chair with a painfully upright back in front of Moffat's expansive desk, behind which Moffat sat in padded splendour in his seat. Moffat was studying papers in front of him.

'A lot of man-hours expended already on this case, which will be dwarfed by what you're requesting now.'

Blades did not answer. When Moffat wanted a reply, he would ask a direct question.

'I thought it was a missing person's case.'

Blades could tell by the lift in the voice at the end of the sentence, that was intended as a query and required him to say something.

'Some people go missing because they're dead,' Blades said. He did wish he could resist stating the obvious.

'Am I not supposed to know that?' Moffat said.

Blades stared at the fingers drumming on the desk.

'So, tell me where you are with inquiries so far and where you're going with them.'

Blades gathered his thoughts. Moffat's fingers continued their rhythmic attack on the desk; the sound seemed to fill the room.

'After Emma Simpson was reported missing, we searched the premises where she stayed and did find traces of blood, which suggested Emma might have come to a bad end. Samples of the blood were sent to the Home Office for analysis and it was found to be human, which meant, as you know – you did approve it – we could apply to the court for a warrant to conduct an in-depth search. In the bathroom, we found human flesh in the drain leading from the bath, plus more blood. When the bath was looked at properly, analysis showed it had been used as a place to cut up a body, which means human parts have been transported elsewhere for disposal as they are nowhere in the Roots' house, shop or back garden.'

'Very good,' Moffat said.

Blades tried to avoid giving him a sharp look and had to glance away.

Then Moffat corrected himself. 'Very bad, of course, but the progress is good.'

'Obviously that was what you meant, sir.'

'But you haven't established it was Emma's body that was cut up?'

'It's a reasonable assumption but we found nothing personal of Emma's anywhere near the bathroom to substantiate it.'

'And you haven't found the rest of the body?'

'That's why the request for man-hours, sir.'

'You want to conduct a search over a fifty-mile radius?'

'The last people to see Emma alive were the Roots on the Saturday morning.'

'I suppose you have checked their back garden already?'

'Oh, yes, sir. That was the first thing we did. And found nothing. Now, their movements on the last day we know of when Emma was seen: they said they left at about ten and arrived at Mrs Root's sister's at about five, which has been verified by the sister and her husband, giving the Roots ample opportunity to dispose of body parts en route.'

'It took them long enough to get there. They are the ones who did it then?'

'It's one line of inquiry.'

'An expensive one. Is there anything definite to suggest they killed her?'

'No. And there are other avenues of investigation. Another suspect is her young man, Alfred Duggan, who does have a record, unlike either of the Roots, but not for violence. He's a convicted bigamist. She'd broken with him, and that could conceivably have led to violence which could have gone too far, leading him to cover his tracks.'

'Did he have access to the house?'

'Once the Roots were away, yes. Obviously, we have no body, and no idea of day of death, never mind time, so it's difficult to narrow things down.'

'And might he have disposed of body parts in the area you're requesting the manpower to search?'

'Yes. He could also have dumped pieces of Emma around Birtleby, which is the reason for the search I want to authorise there.'

'And a few man-hours there too.'

'Of course, sir. It's a serious inquiry. A young woman has been murdered.'

'Quite. At least, you have to assume it was the young woman?'

'Yes, sir,' Blades replied.

'And are there any other lines of inquiry?'

'One we haven't followed up yet, though we will. It's been suggested Emma was also seeing a young man by the name of Russell Parkes.'

'And where's he likely to have disposed of Emma? Not somewhere else?'

'He's a Birtleby man,' was all that Blades thought was necessary to reply to that.

'If you can't find the body, it's a problem,' Moffat said.

'Sir?'

'You've got three suspects, two and a half at the moment, but, even if you assemble a case against one of them, nailing them without a body is a problem. So, yes, your request for funds for all these man-hours is granted. As you say, murder is serious. It's the most serious thing we investigate. We need to put maximum effort into it. Oh, and incidentally, the *Birtleby Times*—'

'Sir?'

'I seem to be finding out about progress on this case more quickly through that rag than through your reports.'

'Paperwork always lags behind legwork, sir.'

'Still, it's embarrassing.'

'Yes, sir.'

Blades cursed Musgrave. Why did he have to be so enthusiastic about this case and why did he have to find out about things so quickly?

CHAPTER SIXTEEN

There were now maps on the walls of Blades' office, large-scale maps, and Blades was poring over them along with Peacock.

'That fifty-mile area between Birtleby and Ramshead. Where are the points of interest?' Blades asked of himself as much as anyone, but, as he was there, Peacock answered.

'Too many to search them all properly.'

'You think?' Blades looked at him, then back to the maps. 'We need to prioritise, concentrate on logistical probabilities.' He frowned and continued examining the maps.

He took out a pencil and drew a circle.

'Logan Woods. They would pass that on their route. It's areas like that we need to look at. Isolated but with cover.'

'Falcombe Moor,' Peacock said. 'That was mentioned by Helen Southwick. We mustn't forget that.'

'That's true,' Blades said. He moved his pencil up and beyond Ramshead to Falcombe Moor, and outlined that area. 'The area adjacent to the path they followed, not that

I think they'll find anything there, but it does have to be looked at too.'

'The area beside the road between Birtleby and Ramshead is pretty well cultivated,' Peacock said.

'Which cuts down options, though there are middens at every farm.'

'Why choose one of those though? It's more likely to be found there.'

'When there are isolated areas where it might remain undiscovered for years. Quite so. Areas like Hackett Hill.' Blades traced another line round that. 'And Bishop Woods.' He drew there too.

So, the two men stood, gazing at the map, and muttering and pointing, with Blades marking it with approximations of circles every so often, till, at last, Blades stood back from the map and tutted.

'We've cut it down,' Blades said. 'But it's still going to take for ever. Not that there's anything to be done about that. And Birtleby is still to be searched. It's a pity we don't have a clearer line on our suspects. If we could rule the Roots out, we wouldn't have to bother with half of this.'

'If only, as you say, sir.'

'But we can't. Who knows what happened in that house? I don't yet.'

'If I were a betting man, I would say it's Root,' Peacock said.

'Why?'

'An attractive young woman like Emma close at hand, and a homely wife like Amelia he's tired of. From what neighbours have said about the way he treats Amelia, he's tired of her. And Emma had a lot of life in her by all accounts. From the look of Amelia, it's all been drained from her.'

'But why kill Emma?' Blades asked.

'Passions flare. A quarrel goes wrong?'

'And there is plenty of scope for passions in that household.'

'But he'd have to get Amelia to cover for him.'

'Is she that frightened of him?' Blades doubted that.

The two men were now looking at the map of Birtleby. 'The streets nearest the Roots' to start off with,' he said. 'No one is going to want to lug body parts a long way. Blood might seep out of a bag, or anything. There are enough back gardens and back yards just on that street to take a proper search a while.' Blades drew a circle round the street. 'We start off with streets to the west of Main Street, going ten streets up. Then we cover the area behind it, again ten streets up.'

'Why no further than that?'

'Duggan wouldn't want to be seen. He's having to take a chance with the disposal of this body, but he won't carry any bag too far.'

'Unless he took a car?'

'In which case he probably went right out of town. And our search area could be as wide as the one we have covering the Roots. But I don't think he got rid of the body parts in that way. He might get blood in the car. That's evidence. Duggan would know he'd be suspected. No. He carried Emma about in different bags. He walked about Birtleby, lifting his cap to greet friends, smiling at young ladies, talking to acquaintances, all the while with a bag that contained the bloody remains of his "fiancée" – if he's the one who did it.'

'And some women thought the world of him.'

'A charming fellow.'

Then Blades stepped back from the maps and looked at them from a distance, nodded, walked back up to the map of North Yorkshire and marked out another area, then walked over to his desk and put his pencil down.

'This is going to take weeks if not months, if we do ever get it all done, but it's time to give out the orders now,' he said to Peacock. 'Time to get this job started.'

'Sir,' Peacock replied.

CHAPTER SEVENTEEN

Blades was doubtful from the moment the phone rang. It was too quick. What they were looking for was a needle in a haystack and they would not find that in five minutes. But the call had come in. A suspicious suitcase had been found two streets down from the Roots'. Blades had Peacock drive him straight there. Entry to the back was gained through a side-gate.

It was an inauspicious setting, Blades thought, as he and Peacock strode through. The buildings in this street were old, soot-blackened, back-to-back, terraced houses, and the back yards were nothing but dirt, black dirt, with spiked railings in between, brick washing houses at the bottom of the yard, alongside outdoor closets. People seemed to pile their rubbish in corners here, instead of using the communal middens further down the street. There were broken chairs, rusty mangles, torn bags with old clothes tumbling out of them, and, there, in the corner, against the wall that separated this back yard from the next one, an old brown leather suitcase. It was battered, and there were stickers on it from better times when it had been used to carry belongings on journeys in trains and boats. The thickness of the leather suggested it had been a quality suitcase.

There was what looked like a stain at the bottom, as if something inside was seeping out, or had done. Or had it just knocked against something as it lay there? They would find out when they opened it. But Blades was in no hurry. One thing he could see about this suitcase was that it matched the one described by a witness, the woman who said she'd seen a man lugging a case about with difficulty. This was a large enough suitcase to fit the description, and, if it had been filled with the parts of a young woman, it would have been heavy. As it lay there, pregnant with possibility, Blades noticed one fastening was hanging open, the lock broken as if forced. That might not fit in with what they were expecting to find, but there was one thing Blades was sure of: he would get as much evidence from this bag as he could.

He signalled to Peacock to get his camera out. They started off with photographs of the case in situ, which Peacock duly obliged with. Then fingerprints were taken. Peacock took out his chalk powder and his insufflator. Once the surfaces in view had been well and truly covered in chalk, Peacock took his painstaking photographs of the fingerprints on show. Then the case was turned over and Peacock took fingerprints from those surfaces as well. The constable who had found this had said he had not touched the case, but his fingerprints would be cross-checked with the ones found here anyway.

Blades looked at the windows above him. These buildings were in a bad state, the sashes on the windows needing a coat of paint, and the faces that peered down at Blades were those of a poor couple, pale, and malnourished, but curious, and with eager eyes. What was this going on in their back yard? Why were the police there? Blades knew that when they turned up, rumours always abounded, and some people made themselves scarce. But this couple had not done that. They were wondering: what's in that suitcase? Why are the police interested in an old case?

Blades looked at it. They had reached the moment of truth. He put out his hand and unclicked the fastening on the right, then slowly pulled the lid of the case open, and peered in. Nothing. Nothing at all. Just torn and dirty silk lining. Could this case have contained body parts? There were no signs of blood, but it was something else to be sent off for examination. He felt relieved. Finding the remains of a body would have been a triumph but would have given no pleasure. As it turned out, it was a suitcase that had been discarded because of a broken lock – more detritus from the world they lived in. It had been made use of, then thrown away when no further purpose could be found for it. He supposed in a way that was what had happened to Emma. And at twenty-three, it had been so soon.

He picked up the case. He was not surprised this had been a dead end. This was not an investigation that was going to go quickly. They might find their body in time. They were still difficult to dispose of, even if they were cut into pieces, and this one would probably surface, but it was never likely to have happened as quickly as this.

The men would persevere with their search. The overtime figures, and the costs, would mount up, and Moffat would continue to groan.

CHAPTER EIGHTEEN

When he met with Russell Parkes, Blades took particular
note of the man's appearance. Did it match any
description in the witness statements so far gathered?
Possibly. Blades and Peacock were interviewing Parkes at
his parents' house. They had been reluctant to allow them
to interview Parkes on his own but had in the end acceded.
With a laugh, Russell had brushed away his mother and
father's concerns. He had seated himself in an armchair,
leaned back, crossed one leg over the other, and looked
the part of a debonair young man holding court. Russell
Parkes did not lack arrogance. With a shake of Mr Parkes'
head and a groan from Mrs Parkes, his parents retreated
from the room.

Russell Parkes was about five foot ten, with black hair
and a gold tooth in the right upper part of his mouth, that
gleamed. There was a bit of a dash to the cut of his suit,
and a thick gold chain led to a pocket of his waistcoat
where his pocket watch lay. He wore a gold signet ring
with a black onyx in the centre of it, and Blades noticed
the gleam on Parkes' black leather shoes. This was a young
man who liked to make an impression, but Blades did not
think him as confident as he pretended; his eyes flickered

with uncertainty between Blades and Peacock, despite Parkes' show of a smile.

'How can I help you, gentlemen?' He beamed.

'We're looking for help from you with an inquiry,' Blades said.

Russell raised an eyebrow in answer to that.

'It's about Emma Simpson, the young lady who disappeared. We've been informed that you knew her.'

The smile remained on Russell's face, but it had acquired a stiffness, and the stretched limbs had tensed.

'Ah, Emma. There's still no sign of her?'

'No, and from what we've discovered, we don't think we will find her.'

'You think she's dead?'

Blades studied Russell. Was that an act? After Musgrave's recent article, Blades was sure everyone thought Emma had been murdered. Perhaps this affable young man did not read newspapers; he did not strike Blades as being especially bright.

'It's a strong possibility.'

'I'm sorry to hear that. So, how can I help you?'

'You did know Miss Simpson?'

'Slightly.'

'Define slightly, sir.'

Russell repressed a laugh, scratched his head, then, realising he had done that, laid his hand on the arm of his seat.

'Let's see. We'd seen each other once or twice. I treated her to afternoon tea once and accompanied her to the pictures on another occasion. She was an attractive young woman, but I had the impression she had someone else in her life.'

'Would you know who?'

'I can't help you there.'

'Do you know her other friends?'

'I didn't get to know her all that well. Chance would have been a fine thing.'

'She gave you the brush off.'

'If you like to put it that way, yes.'

'And how did you feel about that?'

Russell had to think for a moment. 'Disappointed?' he replied.

'Can you tell us about your movements on Saturday the fifteenth?'

Blades could not help but notice the indignation as it gathered in those poised features.

'And why would you ask me that? What would I have to do with Emma's disappearance? The first I knew of it was when my mother pointed out it had been mentioned in the *Birtleby Times*.'

No. Russell Parkes did not read the newspapers himself. 'If that's correct, you won't object to telling me about your movements?'

The expression on Russell's face was now puzzled.

'I won't?'

'As you're innocent, you've nothing to hide.'

'I suppose.' He paused for thought, then continued. 'All right. I was with someone else all day. I went out to lunch with her and then we went for a walk in the park. There was a band playing at the bandstand and we stopped and listened to that.'

'Would you name this person?'

'Rose. Rose Weller.'

'And where could we get in touch with her?'

Russell told him.

'When Emma gave me the "brush off" that's what I did about it. I asked someone else out. I didn't kill Emma – or abduct her. All right?'

Russell's voice was quiet, but no effort was made to hide the anger in it, not that this meant innocence, Blades knew. He had heard that convincing note from felons before.

'Oh, another thing. Why did you leave the Leighton Insurance Company?'

There was a flustered look on Russell Parkes' face as his mind searched about for an answer to that.

'Why would you want to know?' he asked.

'We were told you left under a cloud?'

'I left for a better job. The Prudential's a better company.'

'You landed on your feet. Well done. It must have been a relief.'

'Who's been saying what to you? Because it sounds like rubbish.'

'There were problems with your accounts? It sounded lucky you weren't reported to the police. Or did you pay the money back and resign from the company in return for not being prosecuted?'

Parkes was now seated bolt upright on his chair, his knuckles white as he clenched his fists.

'I deny all of this,' he said.

'It would be easy enough to check with the Leighton Insurance Company.'

Russell had no answer to that. He just stared back at Blades. Then Peacock added his tuppence worth.

'It's also true that you have gambling debts, isn't it?'

'What? How did you know that? All right, some, but not enormous ones. I'll get them worked out.'

'You like a flutter on the horses, though? You go down to the racetrack regularly?' Peacock continued.

'It's not illegal,' Russell replied. 'What makes it any business of yours?'

Peacock did not reply to that, but it was Russell's eyes that moved away.

'And, as you say,' Blades said, 'it's not against the law to bet on horses – and Leighton Insurance hasn't preferred charges against you. I should warn you against running up debts, though. It can lead to difficult situations where it could become our business.'

Then Blades stood up to leave. On the way back to the car, he spoke to Peacock. 'How did you know about the gambling debts?'

'I didn't, sir, but we do now.'

Blades laughed.

'And the fact he bet on horses?'

'It was either that or the dogs. I happened to get it right.'

Blades laughed again.

'Very good. Of course, money had nothing to do with Emma's death, as far as we know. There's no money missing from the Roots' place and Emma didn't have any.'

'There is that,' Peacock replied.

'But he's a suspect.'

'He is?'

'His alibi is a girlfriend. How suspicious is that?'

'Quite.'

Peacock engaged gear and drove off.

CHAPTER NINETEEN

The witness who had called into Birtleby Station was nervous. He was a youngster and he was standing at Sergeant Ryan's desk with an older man, presumably his father.

'Tell him,' said the man, whom Sergeant Ryan was to discover was called Stan Atkinson.

Stan was a stout, bewhiskered, balding man of middle age. He wore a rumpled suit and battered bowler. His shoes were worn down at the heel. But he had an earnest look to his face. This man was trying to be helpful about something.

The boy was about fourteen, skinny as a rake, with ginger hair, a face covered in freckles, and a long, hooked nose. The embarrassed look on his face was pronounced.

'Speak up, Alan. We can't hear you,' boomed Stan.

Alan struggled to find his voice at all, and the man had to speak for him.

'He's a butcher's boy is Alan. Apprenticed to Hogg in Victoria Road.'

'I know the one,' said Sergeant Ryan.

'And he saw something you'll want to know about, didn't you, Alan?' Then Alan's father gave Alan a nudge which almost unbalanced him.

'Yes. Yes. That's right.'

'So, tell him, Alan.' And the boy opened his mouth, but, before he could speak, his father did. 'He doesn't do deliveries usually. He's an apprentice, but he has some to do – Saturday mostly – because it's so busy. And it was on the Saturday that girl disappeared that he saw it.'

'Saw what?' Blades asked.

But it was as if Stan was not listening. He had his tale to tell and he would stick to that.

'He was sure it was a different week. He's no idea of time. A different week? He doesn't know what day of the week it is. Lives his life in a dream, he does. But it was that Saturday, the fifteenth, and that's when he was taking sausages to the Briggs in the Main Street. That's what you were doing that day, wasn't it?' He gave Alan another dig, and Alan nodded this time. 'But he didn't think he could have seen anything. He's no confidence in himself at all, Alan. I keep telling him to take more pride in himself. That's the way to be noticed in this world and get on. But he still doesn't think he could have seen anything that mattered, not that it takes any talent to do that. If a person's in the right place at the right time completely by accident, anyone can see anything, can't they? And you did, didn't you, Alan?'

And Alan had to nod.

'Tell the gentleman,' his father boomed.

Then Sergeant Ryan and the boy's father stared at Alan while he looked back from one to the other and blinked. He opened his mouth again, and, not being interrupted this time, started to speak.

'I'd just turned the corner into Main–'

Then he stopped as if searching for the right way to put things.

'Don't finish now,' his father said. 'You're getting us going here.'

A peevish look came over Alan's face and words started to explode out of him.

'I'll tell you if you give me the chance.'

'Just be patient with him,' Sergeant Ryan said. 'He'll speak in his own time, won't you, Alan?'

Alan looked in a fierce way from one to the other, then nodded his head. 'I'm telling you,' he said. 'I'm telling you.'

Sergeant Ryan and Alan's father waited again.

'He was coming out of the Roots' door,' Alan said. 'I'd never seen him before, and I wondered what he was doing there, but I minded my own business. I didn't say anything to him.'

'Who was coming out of the Roots' door?' Ryan asked.

'A man.'

'What did he look like?' the sergeant asked.

'Tall. With a hat on. When he opened the door, he looked all around before coming out. He did see me but didn't think I mattered or something. Most people don't. But he seemed nervous and I noticed him because of that. And he had two suitcases in his hands.'

Ryan's heart sank at the mention of the suitcases. Maybe this wasn't new information. Maybe this was something to do with the suitcase they'd already found, though the boy had said two, not one. Was that crucial?

Well wound up by now, the boy chatted on. 'I wondered if he was a burglar, then thought, no. I must have got that wrong. He's just setting out for somewhere. Though I knew he wasn't one of the Roots. I know what they look like. But I don't suppose there's any reason why I should know who's staying at the Roots' or not. I thought he must be some visitor, a relative or something.'

'Do you know what time this was?' Ryan asked.

'I'd just passed the town clock and it was just after eleven. I remember noticing because it meant I was in fine time with my deliveries.'

'Can you tell us anything about the suitcases?' Ryan asked.

'They weren't a pair. One was bigger than the other. They were both brown, I think. One was darker. They were both a bit battered. And they were heavy. It was an effort for him to lug them about. And I couldn't help wondering what he had in them.'

'Did they have luggage stickers on them?'

'Dunno. Oh, yes, I suppose, when I think of it, they had.'

'You don't remember what they said?'

'No. It was him I was looking at. He was scary the way he was looking around him.'

'Can you tell me any more about him?'

'He had funny eyes.'

'Funny eyes? In what way?'

'I don't know. I just remember thinking that.'

'Funny eyes.' Oh no, Ryan thought. Not someone else who thought they had seen someone with the eyes of a murderer. Was this another fantasy? Probably.

'So, where did he go after leaving the house?'

'Up the street.'

'Which direction?'

'Towards the square. But I had my rounds to do. I cycled past him and delivered my sausages. Didn't I say? I was on my bike. I only had a glance at him, which was what was odd, that I noticed him at all when I was passing him quickly like that. But he was strange. Though I didn't want to come forward and cause trouble. I didn't want to waste your time.'

'You haven't done that, lad,' Sergeant Ryan said. 'This could be a great help to us. We'll get you to put that in a statement.'

'A statement?'

'Don't worry. I'll write it all down for you and you just have to check it.'

'Then you sign it, son,' his father said. 'Do you see?' he said to Sergeant Ryan. 'I told you it was important. I was right, wasn't I?'

'Oh yes, sir.'

'He could have seen the murderer, couldn't he?'

'Possibly,' Ryan replied. 'Definitely someone we'd want to interview. Now, Alan, you try to think a bit harder about what that man looked like.'

Ryan made his preparations to take the statement.

CHAPTER TWENTY

When Blades and Peacock approached the newspaper seller, he was in full cry. He was a little man, but that voice seemed to fill the street, even if what it was caterwauling out was indecipherable. He was yelling something that sounded a bit like 'Cwawinow', and may have started off as come and buy a newspaper or something of the sort, though it did not sound much like it now. The call did draw the attention of passers-by. One gent bought a *Times*. Then the cry of 'Cwawinow' echoed again down the street, then again. And would have continued had Blades not given the man an authoritarian glare and said, 'We'd like to speak with you,' as he brandished his card.

'If it's about my pedlar's licence, I'll just get it out to show you – when I can find it,' the man said, as he put the newspaper that was in his hand back onto the pile beside him so he could start searching his coat pockets. He was as unprepossessing a person as anyone might care to meet. His hair was lank and greasy, and his coat had seen better days. He had a sniffle which he tried to quell by rubbing his sleeve against his nose.

'It's not about your licence,' Blade said.

'Though it might be the next time,' Peacock said.

'It might?' The newspaperman looked warily at Peacock.

'Though I'm sure it's in order,' Blades said, and his tone was mollifying. 'You were good enough to come into Birtleby Police Station with information.' Blades gave the man a smile.

Then a light dawned with him. 'Ah, that,' he said. And he smiled. 'Only too pleased to help.'

Blades had been interested in the statement the delivery boy had made to Sergeant Ryan but was even more struck by the fact someone else had come into the station saying they had seen a man answering that description at about the same time. The other witness was called Reg Bright, and he sold newspapers in the Main Street at the corner where it met up with the Hainsworth Road, a very handily situated spot to see things associated with the Emma Simpson inquiry, which was why Blades was interviewing him.

The cobbled street was busy. It was a typically Victorian-built street with high, stone buildings on either side, and with tall, ornate streetlamps in black metalwork. There were black railings too in front of the residential houses that lined one side of it. Opposite was a row of shops with broad windows showing wares of differing types under painted wooden signage. Striped awnings jutted out over the windows, to shield the goods from any sun there might be. A coal cart drawn by two weary-looking horses rumbled past, the driver's face almost as black as the coal in the wagon he drove. A motor bus rumbled past after that. A Morris Oxford clattered past in the other direction. Pedestrians walked past. Blades was wondering if Reg would be able to give a better description than Alan of the man he had seen.

'He came out of that door like someone trying to avoid a sniper's bullet.'

'What do you mean?' Blades asked.

'Looking all around him before stepping out, then keeping close to the wall as if looking out for cover.'

Blades supposed he must be exaggerating.

'Was he someone you'd seen before?' Blades asked.

Reg thought for a moment. 'Never seen him before in my life.'

'And what day was this?' Blades asked.

'The Saturday.'

'The fifteenth.'

'And can you say what time it was?'

'There's no point in asking me anything about time. I don't even have a pocket watch. But let's see. About the middle of the day. Mid-day?'

'Have you sold newspapers on this corner for long?'

'A couple of years.'

'Always in the same position?'

'It's a good spot. I catch people going in a couple of directions here. And I'm easy to see. It's a grand place for selling.'

'He's not someone you've seen before going in and out of that house?'

'Not that I've noticed. And I would.'

There was a definiteness in the tone that appealed to Blades.

'Was there anything distinctive about him?'

'A slouch hat. A waistcoat and jacket. Grey.'

'That's good,' Blades said.

'I couldn't tell you the colour of his hair. He was wearing a hat. I did notice he had a particularly pale skin. Not like someone who worked outside or anything.'

'Height?'

'Tall. Not a six-footer like you, though. A couple of inches shorter maybe.'

'No moustache or beard?'

'He was clean-shaven. It was odd the way he kept his head slanted down as if he didn't want to be seen properly. All the same, he somehow managed to take care to look about him, wanted to know everything that was going on. So, I couldn't help noticing his eyes.'

'Why do you mention those?'

'I'm trying to think about that.'

'You wouldn't see the colour of them from that distance?'

'Now, that might be what was funny about them. As if they weren't the colour you might be expecting or something. I don't know. I'm talking rubbish I think.'

'Just describe what you saw.'

A picture of odd eyes had come into Blades' mind, the odd eyes of Alfred Duggan, that piercing blue with the unusual streak of brown in the cornea, and the curious light that seemed to shine through them. Was that what Reg Bright was trying to describe? An oddness that he was aware of but couldn't define, but that Blades, who had studied Duggan from a much closer range, could?

'Would you recognize the man?'

Reg scratched his chin. 'Dunno. Maybe,' he said after a few moments.

'You said he was carrying cases,' Peacock said.

'That's right. Two of them. They looked heavy. I did wonder what might be in them. They'd too much weight for overnight clothes. Though how would I know? I didn't get the chance to look in them, did I?'

'Could you describe the cases?' Peacock asked.

So, Reg Bright did. And he must have had a good look at them, because his description was precise, and they sounded remarkably like the ones described by young Alan Atkinson. We know what we're looking for, Blades thought. He pondered the fact this investigation seemed to be revolving round suitcases. There had been a famous murder inquiry the year before when a suitcase – with a body in it – had been found underneath a seat in an empty railway carriage on the London to Eastbourne line. It had generated numerous newspaper stories as the finder, a middle-aged woman from Croydon who was travelling with twins, had made the most of selling 'exclusive' stories to different newspapers. What had made the story even more famous was the fact the murderer had never been found. Was that story why witnesses in this investigation kept remembering suspicious people with suitcases? It could be. Or, it could have given the murderer the idea of using one to transport the remains of his victim. The suitcase they had tracked down already in this case had been a dead end, but that didn't mean this would be one. If they did turn up Emma's body, and if Alan Atkinson and Reg Bright could pick out Alfred Duggan in an identity parade, then they could be heading for a trial.

CHAPTER TWENTY-ONE

'Do you have anything we could remotely consider taking to court?'

Moffat's look was impatient, which Blades found curious as, despite the latest moment of hope, he knew full well they could still be near the beginning of a complex inquiry.

'We have managed to establish what the crime is by now, I suppose?'

Blades sometimes thought Moffat delivered sentences in his direction like torpedoes. It could be said it had been obvious from the beginning Emma had been murdered, but he supposed what Moffat meant was whether they had proof that was what had happened.

'We have two witnesses who saw someone leaving the Roots' house at about eleven on the morning of the last day that Emma was seen alive. That person was carrying two heavy suitcases. There is human blood in the parlour and in the bathroom. The outlet from the bath contained human flesh. The bath, when examined, showed cut marks consistent with a body being sawn up. It doesn't take much to work out those suitcases contained Emma's remains, which were being taken somewhere to be disposed of.'

'It's an argument,' Moffat said, 'but it's circumstantial, and there's no body.'

'I believe it'll convince a jury we're investigating the murder of Emma Simpson, sir.'

'Without the corpse? Are you sure? And do you have a case against any of the suspects we discussed?'

'Not without an identity parade, no, which we are arranging.'

'And who are the witnesses?'

'A butcher's boy and a newspaper seller.'

'Do their descriptions tally?'

Blades took out his notebook to refer to it.

'Alan Atkinson, delivery boy, states he saw a man with a hat on who was quite tall. He was a man with "funny eyes".'

'Not the best description ever.'

'Mr Reginald Bright, newspaper vendor, states he saw a man in waistcoat and jacket and wearing a hat. He was clean-shaven with pale skin. There was something "funny" about the eyes as if they weren't the colour you might be expecting.'

'And I bet he died with embarrassment after venturing that description.'

'All the same, sir, we have a suspect whom both descriptions might fit – Alfred Duggan. Tall, lean, wears a hat. Might or might not wear a waistcoat, though we could search his wardrobe to confirm.'

'Everyone wears a hat. If he'd been a man not wearing a hat that might have been more helpful.'

'And, having met Alfred Duggan, I can testify to the fact he has "funny eyes".'

'You can?' Moffat gave Blades a questioning look.

'The colour is odd.'

'Didn't they see him from a distance? They wouldn't notice the colour of his eyes unless they were close up to him, if then.'

'Duggan's eyes are a striking shade of blue and, on top of that, there's a streak of brown in the cornea of both that is odd and very noticeable.'

'Which doesn't change my argument.'

'He's used to holding people's attention with those eyes. When he looks at people, they notice it, probably without realising what it is they're noticing.'

'Vague and unconvincing, Blades. I thought you were better than that.'

'Perhaps I'm not describing it well, sir, but both witnesses describe someone with funny eyes and that's what he has.' Moffat looked at Blades with a pitying expression. 'And, if they pick him out in an identity parade, it doesn't matter what you think of that description of him. We do have a suspect we could put in one.'

Blades and Moffat now glared at each other, Blades with defiance. Then Moffat, Blades noticed, could not resist a slight smile.

'Don't mind me, Blades. It's my job to question you. If you can justify yourself to me, you might even convince a jury when a counsel is doing his best to make you sound as unreliable as possible. But I wouldn't go with that description of those eyes in court.'

'Sir.'

'And so, on to the bigamist. I wonder what would have made him kill her?'

'We may never know the answer to that. We can speculate. She said no to something. He became frustrated, they had an argument, he struck out, and the blow or blows killed her.'

'Then he has to cover up.'

'Fortunately, we don't have to prove what's in someone's head. If he killed her, we know there was some sort of motive. That's enough.'

'Thank God for that. It's difficult enough just proving what they did. Still, you've suggested a kind of reason for the murder. Did he have the means?'

'We don't know what killed her at the moment. But there was an obvious disparity in size and strength between them.'

'And opportunity?'

'She was on her own in the house after the Roots left. We know he knew her. She would definitely have allowed him entry if he'd called. If our witnesses do place him there about eleven, carrying those suitcases, opportunity is proven.'

'Then you'd better arrange your identity parade.'

'Sir.'

'But find the body.'

Blades repressed a groan as he left Moffat's office; he knew he had acquitted himself badly.

CHAPTER TWENTY-TWO

Peacock was seated in the room that had been prepared for the identity parade. The looks he was casting in Blades' direction were no less discouraging than Moffat's had been.

'It's difficult enough finding six people answering a physical description, never mind checking if they have peculiar eyes. What does "funny eyes" mean, anyway?' Peacock said.

Blades was tiring of that expression himself. 'You were there when the witnesses were questioned, so you tell me,' was his response.

'The witnesses didn't know what they meant.'

'But they both said the same thing.' Blades hoped his face held an expression that contained more confidence than he felt.

Opposite them stood six young, lean men, and none of them, as far as Blades could see, had strange eyes except Alfred Duggan, who was standing there in what was obviously a cold sweat. His eyes looked shifty as well as odd as they flicked nervously about. The eyes of the other five 'suspects', he knew, had different colours, brown, grey, blue – even green – none of which stood out in any way, and, from where he was sitting now, Blades could not swear to the colour of anyone's.

Blades looked gloomily ahead as Alan Atkinson was led in by Sergeant Ryan. Alan studied every man in the line, then walked back to the fifth man, laid his hand on his chest, then stepped back and away. Blades looked down at the notes in front of him. Who was that man? Ernest Snodgrass, car mechanic, with no known links to either the Roots or to Emma Simpson, and, what's more, who was working in a garage on the day of her disappearance, which was testified to by three different people. Blades shook his head and looked at the floor.

Alan was led out of the room and Reg Bright was led in. There was a nonchalance to him as he walked past the men. Was he taking this seriously? Perhaps it was just a welcome break from standing on a corner selling interminable newspapers. Then, having walked from one end of the row to the other too quickly as far as Blades was concerned, Reg proceeded to walk back down it again at a slow pace that Blades could find no fault with, but with brows which were now furrowed with uncertainty. Blades had decided the identity parade had failed again when Reg turned, walked smartly to Alfred Duggan, stopped in front of him and placed a decisive hand on his chest. Then Reg stepped back and Sergeant Ryan led him out of the room. A defeated look appeared in the 'funny eyes' of Alfred Duggan.

Blades sat back with a satisfaction on his face that stayed there only briefly. 'That might mean nothing,' he muttered.

'Sir?' Peacock replied.

'As you said, how do you find six people with peculiar eyes for an identity parade? There was nothing strange about anyone else's.'

'It's a positive witness identification.'

'But I can't take him to trial on that. If both witnesses had picked him out, maybe. But they didn't.'

'It doesn't mean it wasn't Duggan.'

'That's for sure. He's the most suspicious character we've come across. He didn't care about what he did to any of the women he double-crossed, and that's typical of a killer's mind as well as a bigamist's.'

'He's capable of it.'

'But has no record of violence,' Blades muttered. He stood up and strode from the room.

CHAPTER TWENTY-THREE

Because new information had come to light, Blades decided to interview Russell Parkes again. He interviewed Parkes at the Prudential Office to cause maximum embarrassment.

'He's in this morning,' the middle-aged woman at reception had told Blades and Peacock when they arrived and asked for him – as Blades had previously ascertained their suspect would be. Her look was decidedly wary as she showed Blades and Peacock into the office which Parkes shared with another man. As they entered, Parkes looked up from a desk covered in papers that seemed to amount to columns of figures as much as anything else, presenting a picture that reminded Blades of his first meeting with Duggan.

'Is there anywhere private we can speak, sir?' Blades asked.

'I can go,' the other man said, and rose from his desk. 'Don't mind me. I can catch up with this later. It's about time to start my round for today anyway.'

So, Blades and Peacock were left alone with Parkes, who had not had the time to compose himself into the pose of dashing young man they had encountered before.

His face held a frown, and there was a flustered look in his eyes. Blades allowed himself to stare at those. Russell Parkes had an attractive face with black hair and high cheekbones, and the deep brown eyes would be considered equally attractive by a young woman, Blades supposed, and not in the least 'funny' by anybody, which was a pity as Parkes fitted the description given by witnesses in terms of height and body build. The only thing striking about him was the gold tooth, which gleamed in the light from the window, but no witness had described someone with that feature. Parkes gathered his composure, leaned back in his seat and gestured to an empty chair. He gave a careful smile, as the tooth glinted again.

'How can I help you?' he said, and the tone was welcoming, if the run-of-the-mill eyes looked cold.

'You knew Emma Simpson rather better than you said.'

'Did I?'

'If you tell the truth straight away instead of being caught out in lies, it's a lot less suspicious,' Peacock said.

Parkes' eyes swivelled to meet those of Peacock, before he turned to Blades.

'Who have you been talking to?' he asked Blades.

'We'll ask the questions,' Blades said. 'We would like you to tell us the exact details of your relationship with the murdered woman.'

'Fully and frankly,' Peacock added.

'As I've told you before, there isn't much to tell.'

'You only met up with her twice?' Peacock said, and his face held a measure of contempt that Blades considered ought to be intimidating enough.

Parkes shrugged in an over-deliberate attempt at continuing his nonchalance. 'So, it was three times?' His eyes did succeed in holding those of Blades.

'Much more than that,' Blades replied.

Then Parkes did look away.

'I would consider your answers more carefully,' Peacock said.

Parkes considered.

'All right, we had a shared interest in music,' he said. 'We used to meet up and play for each other.'

'Very proper,' Peacock said.

'It was. She came around to my parents' house several times and we played music for each other. I play the violin and Emma played the piano.'

'And were your parents there at the time?' Blades asked.

'Usually.'

'But not always.'

'They were out once.'

'So, an intimate relationship?' Blades asked.

'Not in the sense you mean.'

'But if you had turned up at the Roots' house when Emma was by herself, she would have admitted you?' Blades said.

'That's not what happened.' There was now a fierce expression in Russell Parkes' eyes, and his jaw was set at a defiant angle.

'We know you have debts,' Blades said. 'You didn't go around in the hope of getting any money out of Emma?'

Now Parkes laughed. 'She didn't have any.'

'But there might have been money in the Roots' house,' Peacock said.

'Not that I know of,' Parkes said.

'You didn't happen to have an argument with Emma about that, I suppose?' Blades asked.

'That ended up in killing her? Certainly not. I think you should drop this, and try to find the person responsible for Emma's disappearance, don't you?'

Blades noted that Parkes' voice had risen. He looked at Parkes' face and tried to read the mind behind. Had Parkes killed her?

'Why didn't you tell us about your other conviction, Mr Parkes?' Blades asked. Now there was not the slightest look of the debonair about Russell Parkes. 'Just because it took place elsewhere didn't mean we wouldn't find out about it.'

'You assaulted a young woman,' Peacock said.

'I don't sexually assault women. Women find me attractive. Why would I do that?'

'As you know, it wasn't a sexual assault,' Blades said.

'It was an argument about money,' Peacock added.

'You were in debt again,' Blades said, 'and the young woman wouldn't agree to hand over savings to you.'

'All right,' Parkes replied. 'That happened then. It didn't happen with Emma Simpson.' Now his eyes looked desperate. 'Oh, go bother somebody else,' he said. 'Don't keep on hounding me about something that happened in the past.'

'We're not hounding you,' Blades said. 'We're exploring your connection with a murdered woman, Emma Simpson.'

It was a nice theory was what Blades was thinking. But there had been no signs on the Roots' premises of any hunt for money, and no report from the Roots about any missing, nor had there been any present on the property, which didn't mean Parkes and Emma hadn't argued about money. Had he wanted Emma to get some for him?

'Well, you know about it now. We shared an interest in music.'

He glared back at Blades who returned the look. Russell Parkes could have done this or not, but he had lied. And, in Blades' experience, people who told untruths in murder investigations had something to hide.

CHAPTER TWENTY-FOUR

'Moffat's threatening to call off the search for the body in Birtleby.'

When Blades had walked into the office, tossed his hat onto the coat-stand, and sloughed off his overcoat before discarding it in the same place, Peacock had studied him with alarm. Blades' mood was written all over him and it was not good.

'Don't let him, sir,' Peacock replied.

'We can't. We haven't covered half the area,' Blades said.

Peacock grunted. He also knew how much they needed to find that body.

'Is he ending it?' Peacock asked Blades.

'At the moment, it's a threat,' Blades said. 'Some helpful pressure.' Blades walked over to his desk and slumped into his seat. His eyes swept over the papers sitting there, before he directed his gaze at Peacock, seated at his desk.

'How about the search between Birtleby and Ramshead?' Peacock asked.

'That's under threat as well,' Blades said, 'though he might give it longer as we're covering a wider area.'

'He thinks it more likely the Roots did it than Duggan?'

'He didn't say that, but he doesn't think we've paid enough attention to them.'

'We've no real evidence the Roots had anything to do with it.'

'Nothing else has turned up to incriminate them but that might not mean anything. Something could have been going on between Thomas Root and Emma – which led to an argument, which led to Emma's death.'

'And a cover-up which we don't think Amelia Root would agree to be complicit in?' Peacock said.

'It's not likely,' Blades replied. 'Though how likely is anything? Nobody who was acting in a sensible way would kill anyone.'

'Do we have corroboration for any naughty business between Thomas and Emma? Nobody's come forward with information there was anything going on between them.'

'Who's been asked?' Blades said, before answering his question himself. 'The daily maid was interviewed.' He lifted a file from the shelf behind his desk and sifted through it. 'Here it is. Sergeant Ryan talked with her. Louisa Fleetwood, twenty-four, 18 Northcliffe Road.'

'Why didn't we see her ourselves?'

'We were too busy. We were following up on Russell Parkes as we'd been told by Musgrave and Duggan.'

'Helpful of them.'

'There's a full statement from Louisa, though, from what I remember, there's little in it.' Blades ran his eyes over it again. 'She says, "Thomas Root's a model employer who treats staff with respect and courtesy, pays on time, and doesn't give employees excessive workloads." Not a whiff of complaint about him in anything she said.'

'Not one moan?'

'No.'

'Not about Amelia either?'

'No.'

'So, what did she say about Emma?'

Blades perused the page. 'She did have a go at her. Thought she was a bit flighty and had ideas above her station. She was up to no good with that Alfred Duggan. Everyone knew all about that.'

'When she said that everyone knew, did that include anyone who spoke to us?'

'The Roots?'

'But nobody else. So, what was she on about?'

'You might ask.' Blades looked thoughtfully at Peacock. 'Louisa is Thomas Root's second cousin on his mother's side.'

'Is she?'

'She might defend the good Thomas as he's family.'

Blades could almost see thoughts racing through Peacock's mind now. 'Did she have a prejudice against Emma? She didn't have a thing about Thomas herself, did she?'

'And Thomas was interested in Emma but not her?' Blades suggested.

'And Louisa was piqued about that.'

Then Blades closed the file with a snap. There was a look of disgust on his face. 'We're speculating. There's nothing in the files that gives us any more to question Thomas Root about. Which is what Moffat wants us to do, but we would need something else to give us a way in, or the interview would go the way of the previous one – nowhere. If body parts were turned up en route, that would help.'

'Their car was clean when it was searched?'

Blades shuffled some more of the papers on his desk.

'Absolutely. Of course, we don't suspect the murder was carried out in the car. We only think the body might have been transported in it – in suitcases maybe – and they could have had a tarpaulin down under that.'

'There wasn't one in the car?'

'No, but that could have been dumped with the cases.'

Blades peered again at the papers on his desk. There were enough of them. He could hope one of them would help.

'There's no report from anyone of seeing a suspicious-looking couple dumping anything from a car between Birtleby and Ramshead?' Peacock asked.

'No.'

Blades took out a packet of Woodbines, offered one to Peacock, and lit his own and Peacock's. He breathed in smoke and allowed it to fill the lungs fully before he exhaled. He allowed his eyes to dwell on his sergeant. He supposed the expression on his own face mirrored that on Peacock's – baffled frustration.

'We'll interview Louisa again,' Blades said. 'That might give us something to task Thomas Root with.'

'I look forward to that,' Peacock said.

Both men drew in smoke from their cigarettes as they pursued their own thoughts.

'How much longer is Moffat allowing for the search?' Peacock asked.

'He didn't say. I wouldn't give it any more than a couple of days.'

'It probably won't matter. The most likely thing is that the body has been washed far out to sea by now,' Peacock said.

'You think so?'

'We've done due diligence, but I'm sure you've worked out as well as I have the best way to get rid of a body around here is at the mouth of the river where it will be carried out to the North Sea.'

'And without a body, how do we progress?' Blades said. He drew in some more cigarette smoke and gave his attention to that, but, despite himself, his thoughts continued to race. Without a corpse, what proof was there a murder had been committed? Could they even show conclusively someone had been killed? His eyes swept over the papers on his desk. There often was a point in a case when they came to the end of their ideas. Usually, they worked their way past it, but he wondered if they would this time. He thought of Emma's parents. They had wanted Emma to be found alive. He stubbed the cigarette out in the metal ashtray on the desk in irritation.

'We should have met up with Louisa Fleetwood and talked to her before now,' he said.

CHAPTER TWENTY-FIVE

Louisa Fleetwood was in the middle of scrubbing the kitchen floor. How did floors get so dirty when maids like her were down on their hands and knees scrubbing at them so regularly? If Amelia Root employed a cook there wouldn't be so much mess. Cooks cleaned up after themselves and hated a dirty kitchen. She had heard Amelia going on to her precious Thomas that her sister had a cook, so shouldn't she have one? Weren't the meals divine when they visited them?

If Mr Root wasn't so interested in saving money for that prosperous retirement he was always talking about, perhaps they could have a prosperous here and now? Louisa Fleetwood agreed with her. Then she might be paid more than starvation wages, and there might be less work for a maid to do when they did call her in. She only came in to do them a favour, she told herself. Her gran thought this was helping out one of her favourites in the family. Thomas was the only one of them all who had done half well. And Gran thought it was helping out Louisa too, which it might have been, though Louisa was sure there must be better jobs around.

Still, there was something about Thomas that drew Louisa. He had a way with him, a sparkle in his eyes, a way of speaking so grandly – and he was a one sometimes. There were times when he caught her in a corner and didn't half give her a cuddle. Of course, it couldn't lead to more than that, and wouldn't – they were related, and he was a married man – but she did sometimes wish she could meet someone like him for herself. All the young men she knew her own age were struggling and broke. They had their way to make and she had never had the luck to meet anyone eligible who had already done that. Forget about that, she thought. Scrub. Scrub. Scrub. Take a pride in this floor, girl, she told herself. Pay attention to what you're doing instead of all this daydreaming. Then another voice in her head reminded her that people would walk all over it, so what was the point in taking too much care? There was the rapping on the front door, and she wondered why someone didn't answer it, before reminding herself she was the maid. Everyone else was far too grand in that house to answer the door. She put her scrubbing brush to the side, pulled herself to her feet, straightened her back, and marched truculently to the door.

There were two men there, neither of whom she recognized. They were both tall. One had a bowler and a tash, the other a flat cap and no tash. They both wore rumpled suits and had tired-looking eyes that gave her speculative looks. What was that about?

'Can I help you?' she said. 'Mrs Root doesn't speak to salesmen at the door, if that's what you're about.'

'You're Louisa Fleetwood?' the man with the tash said.

'So what if I am?' Louisa said, 'And what business is it of yours?'

Moustache man smiled. It was an appeasing smile and Louisa wondered why he was flashing that at her. He fished in his pocket and pulled out a card that he held towards her, but, before she had the chance to read it, introduced himself anyway.

'I'm Inspector Blades, this is Sergeant Peacock, and it's not Mrs Root we want to speak to, it's your good self. May we come in?'

Then he pushed the door further open before she could say anything, and he and the other one walked straight past her. Louisa's heart sank. Blades and Peacock. She had heard about them and thought she had been clever avoiding them before. There was something to be said for part-time work.

'Where would the best place be to talk?' Blades asked.

'I didn't say we could,' Louisa said. 'And I didn't say you could come in either.'

The other one, who must be Peacock, spoke now. 'It's police business,' he said. 'You want to keep in with the police, don't you?'

Louisa thought he had a face a bit like a weasel and didn't take to him.

'I've not done anything wrong,' Louisa replied. 'What do you mean?'

Then the one who had said he was Inspector Blades put on that smile again, which Louisa decided looked more like a grimace, as if he was in pain about something, and, if he was, it was nothing to do with her. With any luck, maybe Mr Root would come down and throw the pair of them out, but until he did, she supposed there was nothing she could do but try and get through this.

'The kitchen, I suppose,' she muttered, and led them through. She'd noticed neither of them had wiped their feet on the mat on the way in and wondered how much mess they would make on the floor she had been working so hard on. But she gestured towards seats round the table and they seated themselves there, as she sat herself down opposite them. She could not help noticing the mud on the boots of the sharp-faced one with the flat cap.

'I've work to do,' she said, 'and I'll be in trouble if I don't get it done. This won't take long, will it?'

That inspector Blades gave her an appeasing look and she tried not to mutter. Peacock weasel-face took out a notebook and pencil. Certainly not much like a peacock, she thought. He was dull grey from top to bottom, with that grey suit and cap, and shirt that had been white once, but seemed to be starting to turn grey too with age. Blades was the one who spoke again.

'According to your statement, Mr Root is a model employer,' he said.

'It's no crime to say that,' she said. 'And he's all right to work for. He's pleasant enough and he pays on time and doesn't bother me.'

She wished he would bother her a bit more, but that was hardly something to tell any stranger, never mind a policeman.

'And how did he treat Emma?' Blades asked.

'I wouldn't know,' Louisa replied. 'I wasn't in their company all the time, but Emma didn't complain about him to me, and he was all right with her when I was around.'

'Would you say Emma was an attractive young woman?' Sergeant Peacock said.

'She wasn't ugly,' Louisa said. 'She did have a young man interested in her.'

'Alfred Duggan?' Blades said, to which Louisa nodded.

'Anyone else?' Peacock said.

'Not that I know of. And she didn't talk of knowing anyone anywhere else. She was no Gloria Swanson. She wouldn't have had a stream of them after her.'

'And what did you think of her relationship with Alfred Duggan?' Blades asked.

'What anyone would. She needed to be careful with the likes of him. That sort's all charm and words and smiles — and hands. There was only one thing he was after and if she had a head on her she'd have seen that.'

'So, did she have a head on her?' Blades asked.

'She thought he was the bee's knees and she'd a good catch. Maybe I should have told her otherwise.'

'What makes you say that?' Peacock asked.

'Something happened to her, didn't it?'

'You think Duggan had something to do with that?' Blades asked.

'Someone did, and he was someone she knew. He could have.'

'You haven't heard him say anything about it?' Peacock asked.

'I've never seen him to ask. I just saw him with Emma a couple of times, that's all, and I thought, God, she'd better watch out for him. It was what he looked like, and it's what I thought of him, but he could be like anything, for all I know. I didn't know him.'

'Young women like yourselves have instincts about men,' Blades said.

'Maybe,' Louisa said. 'We know we've got to watch out for them.'

'Was Thomas Root attracted to Emma?' Peacock asked.

Louisa giggled, then stopped herself.

'Was he?' Blades said.

She had to admit she had caught him leering at Emma too from time to time. 'I suppose – there was a small smile on his face when he looked at her sometimes, as if he wished he was a bit younger, but I doubt if it went past that.'

'You think?' Blades said.

Louisa thought of the times the good Thomas had caught her in a corner and the cuddles he'd given her. 'Just a laugh,' he had said. 'Just bit of fun. You don't mind, do you? Just keep it between the two of us.' And he had given her another cuddle. And she had let him do it for a moment or two before brushing him off and telling him to behave himself and asking what his wife would say. But she had felt sorry for him. She knew he and Amelia had separate bedrooms and doubted if Amelia let him anywhere near her anymore. And Blades must have read something of that in her face because he said, 'There was never a little smile on his face when he looked at you?'

Louisa had choked at that. What would Gran say if she heard about the cuddles? What would Amelia say? And what if the street got to hear about it? She had let him.

'He's a model employer,' she said. 'He's never bothered me.'

'A model employer?' Peacock said. 'That's a stilted way of speaking. That's not what he told you to say, is it?'

'I've answered your questions,' Louisa said. 'Is that it?' She was tired of this. She just wanted them to go.

'You're related to Mr Root, aren't you?' Blades said.

'On his mother's side,' Louisa said. 'But not close. A lot of people around here are sort of related to each other. It's a small town. What of it?'

'Do you feel the need to protect him?' Blades asked.

'What do you mean?'

'Was he up to anything with Emma?' Peacock asked.

'I've told you he wasn't,' Louisa said, and she hoped not. He was her own bit of a giggle.

'So, you have,' Blades said. 'I don't suppose you were around on the Saturday when the Roots left for Ramshead?'

'No. Saturday's not one of my days here.'

'You didn't see Emma on the Saturday or later?' Blades asked.

'No.'

'When was the last time you did see her?'

'It must have been the Friday. I'm here on a Friday morning so I suppose I might have seen her that morning.'

'You suppose you might?'

'All right I did.'

'And how did she seem? Was anything bothering her? Did she seem excited about anything?'

Louisa thought about that. That was the day Emma had told her she had seen her and Mr Root in one of their corners and she'd said she'd tell. Louisa remembered that all right. It had been a nasty little argument and Louisa had been the one on the receiving end.

'She seemed just the same as usual,' Louisa said.

Louisa remembered wondering why Emma had been so vehement. Was Emma really being a Miss Goody Two Shoes or did she have a thing going with Thomas herself? She asked herself if she should mention that suspicion to this inquisitive detective but for the moment at least something held her back.

CHAPTER TWENTY-SIX

Thomas Root now walked into the kitchen. When he saw Blades and Peacock were questioning Louisa, the interrogative look he flashed at them was chilling. On seeing her employer, Louisa blurted out, 'I didn't tell them anything.'

'What might you have told us?' Peacock said, pulling his notebook and pencil out again.

'Oh, I didn't mean–' The flustered Louisa looked from Blades to Peacock to Thomas Root then back again with an open but now silent mouth.

'It's all right, Louisa,' Thomas said. 'So, what is it you've been asking Louisa about?' he asked Blades.

Blades had been unhappy with the interview of Louisa as, at the end of it, they had discovered nothing about Mr Thomas Root to question him with, but he supposed the moment had now come and they would be having a go at him anyway. And there was now that remark of Louisa's that could be followed up on. But he would interview Thomas Root on his own.

'Thank you, Louisa. We've finished with you just now.'

In reply to this, Louisa looked round at what was her own workplace, as if wondering why she was the one who should be leaving it, but tramped out anyway, a sullen look on her face.

'What is it Louisa was not supposed to tell us?' was Blades' reply.

'I don't know of anything,' Thomas said, 'so I've no idea what she meant by that. I'm not so sure she does. You're the police. You're intimidating. She was probably just worried about the way anything she said might be interpreted.'

'Such as?' Blades asked.

Thomas ignored that. 'So, what progress have you made apart from terrifying my maid?'

Blades noticed the way Thomas was now trying to lead the conversation. 'You're sure there was nothing definite Louisa was told not to tell us?'

'And now you're insulting me. I'm quite sure, and I can't imagine what that might conceivably have been. Look, an employee of mine, Emma Simpson, is missing and I'm anxious about her. What have you done to trace her and what do you think has happened to her? I would like to know.'

If Thomas was determined not to answer the question properly, Blades was not sure what more he could do about it but he did not like being interrogated about the investigation.

'The search continues for Emma's body,' was all he said.

'No nearer to finding that?'

'No.' Blades studied Thomas's face. 'What kind of young woman would you say Emma was?' he asked him.

'I don't know what you mean,' Thomas replied.

'What did you think of her?'

'She was a good worker.'

'You didn't think past that with her?'

'And what do you mean by that?'

'It's just a question,' Blades replied in a non-committal way.

'She was a determined girl. I noticed that.'

'Determined about what?'

'Anything she did really. She made a success of things.'

'How was she with customers?'

'Pleasant. Polite. Respectful. Helpful. Friendly.'

'So, you did notice a lot about her?'

Thomas showed his irritation with a snort. 'She was an employee. You do. You need to work out whether she's any good at her job or not.'

'And was she?'

'Very.'

'Did the male customers like her?'

'I don't know what you mean.'

'Were there any customers who showed an interest in Emma?'

'She was an attractive young woman, and that wouldn't be wasted on them, but men are usually with their wives when they come in here. They're not going to flirt with staff in front of them. And Emma certainly wasn't encouraged to engage in inappropriate conversations with men.'

'Nobody behaved in an unsuitable way with her?'

'As I've said, no. Not when I was there.'

Now Peacock spoke. 'You say she was attractive. Were you attracted to her?'

Thomas's look at Peacock was unfriendly, and he was obviously biting back a retort.

'You're investigating something, so I suppose I have to accept questions like that.' But he gave Peacock another glare before he continued. 'Emma was an employee, and, at her age, could have been my daughter.'

But the way he said that did not make him sound innocent, Blades thought.

'You said you didn't think Duggan was good enough for her,' Blades said.

'Duggan's a convicted bigamist. He isn't good enough for anybody.'

'You caught her with him acting in an unseemly manner, you said?' Peacock asked.

'She's not getting pregnant on my premises.'

'They'd gone that far?' Peacock asked.

'If Duggan had his way.'

'Did that lead you to think this was a young woman who was up for it?' Blades asked.

'Certainly not.' Though his flustered look suggested he had been struck on a nerve. 'Don't you have anything better to do with police time than waste it in asking questions like that?' Root replied, though Blades thought the self-righteousness was overdone.

'Did it annoy you when she said no to you?' Peacock asked.

Root started to say something but only a splutter came out. He pulled himself up to his full height, still short of either Blades or Peacock, and said, 'That certainly didn't happen. I wouldn't make advances towards staff, or anyone else. I'm happily married. You can ask anyone.'

'We will,' Blades said.

'Definitely,' Peacock agreed.

'And that won't worry me,' Root said.

Which might be true, Blades thought, thinking back to the interview with Louisa, though there was too much bluster here. Did he have a thing going with Louisa? That would explain her protectiveness towards him.

'Did Emma talk about any other young men?' Peacock asked.

'If she had, I would tell you. But she wasn't the flighty type. She had an undesirable boyfriend. That was all.'

Blades left it at that. Root hadn't cleared himself, in Blades' mind, but all they had against him were suspicions without justification for them. Blades supposed he could at least report to Moffat that he had questioned the man.

CHAPTER TWENTY-SEVEN

'Russell Parkes' alibi is false.'

Blades was looking at the sneering face of Musgrave. The reporter had just interrupted them when he and Peacock had been about to motor over to Hantwell Woods, the area that was being searched that day. It was frustrating. Blades had been trying to take charge of his own case.

'You're taking a great deal of interest in this one,' Blades said.

'Aren't you?' Musgrave said.

'Hold on a minute,' Peacock replied.

A smug smile appeared on Musgrave's face.

'You're awfully sure about Parkes' alibi,' Blades said.

'Absolutely,' Musgrave replied. 'Rose Weller works at the Odeon Picture House. She's quite the pianist. Have you never been there when she's on? And she is, every Saturday – all day. She starts off with the Saturday morning cinema for the kiddies.'

'Does she indeed?' Blades turned to Peacock. 'I thought we checked out Duggan's story?'

'Sergeant Ryan. He and Flockhart, they verified it.'

'They talked with Rose Weller, no doubt,' Musgrave said. 'Did they talk with Pat Naismith, the manager of the Odeon?'

'Did they?' Blades asked Peacock.

'Did we know she worked there?' Peacock replied.

'We should have done.' Blades hoped the expression on his face did not look as ineffectual as he felt. 'What led you to this?' Blades asked Musgrave.

'A nose for the truth,' Musgrave boasted. 'Journalists have to do their bit and truth always helps.'

'Their bit?' Blades said.

'You didn't fight in the war, did you?' Musgrave said but continued, giving Blades no chance to reply, 'I learned what duty was then. It applies in peacetime too.'

'Inspector Blades did his bit in the war,' Peacock said. 'How could a country cope without any serving police officers?'

'I suppose,' Musgrave said. 'I didn't mean that–'

'Didn't you?' Peacock said.

Then Musgrave paused. 'A lot of people came back damaged.'

'Damaged?' Blades said.

'Isn't that what this is?'

What was Musgrave leading up to, Blades wondered.

'We get young women going missing like this. And what are the police doing about it?'

'We're working on this case,' Peacock said.

Then Musgrave laughed. 'I was just at the Odeon House to see a picture show, and saw Rose Weller there, on a Saturday.'

'It must be good to have the time to go to the pictures,' Blades said. What he was thinking was that he did not quite get Musgrave and he was wondering why.

'It was useful,' Musgrave said. 'I talked to Pat Naismith. He was happy enough to wax lyrical about his Rose. Very popular she is. Audiences have gone up since she started playing there. And he wouldn't let her have a Saturday off.

It's his busiest day. He was very surprised when I suggested she might have been elsewhere.'

'And have you talked to Rose about that?' Blades asked.

'Not yet,' Musgrave replied.

'We can beat you to something.'

'All right, now give,' Musgrave said.

'What do you mean, give?' Blades replied.

'I've helped you with your job, now you help me with mine. Where are the investigations at the moment?'

Blades thought about the point of despair he had been reaching and did not want to give that publicity.

'Inquiries are ongoing on a number of fronts,' he said. 'It's imperative we find the body.'

'It's still not turned up?'

'Not yet.'

'You won't be able to prosecute without that, will you?'

'That's why killers try to hide the corpse, but I'm not sure it's something they should rely on.'

'Doesn't it mean Emma could still be alive?'

'That would be good news. If anyone has seen her, the information would be invaluable.'

'But why would she not have been in touch before now if she's still alive?'

'Information on that, if known, would also be appreciated.'

'Your investigation hasn't advanced at all, has it? You still don't even know what you're investigating: a missing persons case or a murder?'

'After this length of time, we don't expect to find Emma alive.'

'Have you dismissed Duggan from the investigation?'

'We haven't dismissed anyone.'

'Or done anything?' Musgrave asked.

Musgrave was going a bit over the top here, wasn't he?

'That's not a helpful comment.'

'My readers would like to be assured of the efforts the police have been putting in.'

'Constables have been out searching everywhere in Birtleby for Emma's remains. They've also been searching a wider area outside Birtleby because we have reason to suspect a body could have been disposed of there. Neighbours have been questioned. People who knew Emma have been questioned. Reports that have been received from the public have been followed up. Statements have been taken and checked. A lot of man-hours have been expended on this case and continue to be.'

'And do you know yet how Russell Parkes managed to pay off his gambling debts?'

Blades gave Musgrave what the reporter probably thought was a satisfyingly surprised look.

'And how would you know he owes money to anybody?'

'When I'm not at the cinema, I'm busy digging about. It's my job as a crime reporter.'

'Don't you think you're going a bit beyond that?' Blades said. Musgrave was puzzling him. 'Journalists aren't supposed to be doing the actual job of the police.'

'The work the police ought to be doing, you mean?'

Blades looked at him, non-plussed. Musgrave was not only ahead of them, he was getting ahead of himself.

'Why such an interest in this case?' Peacock asked.

'Some of us are ambitious,' Musgrave replied.

'Aren't we all?' Peacock said. 'We're working on this. I hope you're not going to write we're not.'

'Leave it, Sergeant,' Blades said.

'He's always been happy enough reporting on garden fetes and school sports days before now. He's showing a lot of energy for him.'

'And he's dug up some useful information for us,' Blades said.

'I suppose,' Peacock said, 'but there's no reason to rub our faces in it.'

'I'm sure that's not what you're doing, is it?' Blades said to Musgrave.

There was a cheeky grin all over Musgrave's face, but he did say, 'No offence intended.'

'And none taken,' Blades replied. 'And I suppose we'd better question that witness again.'

'Rose should be on her way to the cinema about now,' Musgrave said.

'Thank you for the information,' Blades said.

Blades opened the door and climbed into the police Ford. Peacock did the same, and they drove off, nowhere near where the search for body parts was ongoing, which was where Blades would rather be, but towards the Odeon, exactly where Musgrave had directed them.

CHAPTER TWENTY-EIGHT

Rose was preparing for the matinee performance when Blades and Peacock came upon her. She was a young woman with pretty red hair, who wore a lurid lipstick, and whose lips curved into a perennial half-smile. She was seated at the piano, perusing sheet music as she did finger exercises on the keys.

The Odeon was a marvel of gaudy velvet curtains and curving rococo plaster figures of cherubs. The red of the curtains and the gold of the cherubs added to the impression of decadent ostentatiousness. The piano itself was a sweeping grand, if the notes sounding out from it were obviously not coming from a Steinway. One or two members of the audience had started to trickle in and were seated together, talking in quiet tones.

Blades and Peacock were striding down the central aisle towards her, with Blades feeling embarrassingly sombre for the setting. She looked up at him from her piano sheets, lips half-open with surprise, eyes gawping as Blades proffered his card.

'Inspector Blades,' he said, 'and this in my colleague, Sergeant Peacock.' Rose continued to stare at them both.

'We'd like to question you about some information you gave to one of our constables.'

'Oh, that,' Rose said, as her expression hardened.

'You've stated that on the Saturday the fifteenth you spent all day in the company of a Mr Russell Parkes.'

'That one,' she said.

'That's right,' Blades said.

'A tall man, with dark hair and a gold tooth on the top right of his mouth,' Peacock added.

Rose give Peacock a quizzical stare in return.

'I remember what he looks like,' she said. 'I don't go out with loads of them.'

'There's something you haven't remembered properly though, isn't there?' Blades said.

'Is there?' Rose was alarmed now and looked as if she might like to make a bolt for it. 'I remember where we went,' she said. 'We had lunch at Pierre's and a very nice lunch it was too. Sole meunière. That Russell Parkes doesn't half give you a good treat. He's no skinflint, I'll say that for him. Followed by a very nice piece of lemon tart. Then we had a walk in the park and listened to the band. It was playing a lovely medley of tunes. Very patriotic some of them were too. Stirring. It was a pleasant day for the park, even if it was so chilly. It was sunny and I was glad I had a broad-brimmed bonnet on. My skin's that pale. It really catches the sun. I'm all freckly now, if you notice.'

'You've got that pat,' Peacock said. 'Did he write all that down so you could learn it up?'

'I don't know what you're talking about,' Rose replied. 'You ought to treat me better than that. I haven't done anything.'

'Not yet,' Blades replied, 'but if you appear in court saying all that, you will be committing perjury and liable to prosecution.'

Rose gaped but said nothing, wisely, Blades thought.

'You work Saturdays,' Peacock said. 'How can you be playing the piano here at the same time that you're going for a walk in the park?'

'Oh,' Rose said.

'It's not even a well thought out alibi,' Blades said. 'Bands don't even play in the park on a Saturday. Who came up with that one? Russell Parkes, I suppose? He can't be bright. Why are you bothering with the likes of him?'

'I must have got the days mixed up,' Rose replied. 'Wasn't it the Friday you were asking about? That's the day we went to the park. And the band was playing that day. I'm off on Friday. I only work the evening then. You can ask anyone. A girl can get mixed up, can't she? That's not breaking the law. You can't charge me with that.'

'So – not the Saturday. You mistook the day in your previous statement.'

'I must have done, mustn't I?' Rose said.

'So, you'll give another statement to that effect,' Peacock said.

Rose was close to tears now, Blades thought.

'If I have to, yes,' she said.

'How did Parkes persuade you to give that alibi?' Blades asked.

'He said it was the Friday. Honest. I thought that was the day you were all talking about. I wouldn't tell any lies to the police.'

Oh really? Blades thought. He looked at Rose carefully. He didn't suppose she earned very much from her stints at the front of house, playing a cinema piano. It might not take very much of a present of money to persuade her to help a friend out when he was being wrongly accused.

'You'll come in tomorrow morning to Birtleby Police Station to give that new statement,' Blades said.

'All right,' Rose said. 'But that'll be it, won't it? You won't be charging me with anything? I don't know what my mum would say, and I might lose my job too.'

'You should have thought of that,' Peacock said.

CHAPTER TWENTY-NINE

When Duggan turned up at the police station again, Blades did not know how to react. They weren't following leads on him at the time but rather on Russell Parkes. Was Duggan trying to point the finger in his own direction?

'I'm sure,' he was saying, 'I'm sure she was seeing someone besides me.'

This was well established, so what was Duggan doing turning up with this?

'You've already suggested she might be seeing Russell Parkes,' Peacock said.

'And I'm saying it again. Look, there were loads of times when I wanted to see her and she was evasive, and, OK, I could see her job took up a lot of time, but–'

'What?' Blades said.

'You didn't know her. You don't know what I mean. She had a way of glancing sideways when she was being caught out on something. If there was a good reason why she couldn't see me, she just looked straight at me, as if teasing me. "Can't see you then. You'll just have to wait" sort of thing.'

'You might be right, I suppose,' Blades said, 'but that sounds hard to verify.'

'I always knew she would come into money.'

'She would?' said Blades, to whom this was news.

'She had an aunt in Leeds, her Aunt Effie; she married late – to a man with a business. When he died, she inherited, and she'd been ill herself for years. Emma was her favourite and she'd always said she would leave everything to Emma.'

'So, why haven't we heard this from her family?'

'She only ever said it to Emma. Only she knew she would inherit everything. Her aunt was afraid of causing jealousies.'

'And how much was everything?'

'How would I know? I don't, but it was thousands.'

Peacock whistled. Blades blinked – several times. It was Peacock who pointed out the obvious.

'So, he killed her for money she hadn't inherited yet? How does that help him?'

'You don't see it. Her aunt died a month ago.'

'She did?' Blades said. 'Emma already had the money?'

'It hadn't come through yet.'

'Which still doesn't help any paramour of Emma's if he's already killed her,' Peacock said.

'You say she was seeing someone else,' Blades said. 'Could there have been someone besides Russell Parkes?'

'I don't know of anyone else. I've seen her and Russell together.'

'Where?' Blades said.

'I saw them walking along the front.'

'When was this?'

'A couple of weeks ago.'

'Not the Saturday of her disappearance?'

'No. You know he was heavily in debt?'

'We'd worked it out,' Blades said. 'You've proof of it?'

'Word on the street. Not proof. No.'

'So, what form did the word on the street take?'

'He was in debt to a turf bookie.'

'Who had a name?'

'Rawlins.'

'I've heard of him. The amiable Geoffrey.'

'That's the one. What I heard was he'd told Russell he would break both of his legs if he didn't pay up by this Friday.'

'I still don't see how Russell can get the money from Emma if she's dead,' Peacock said.

'Unless some money already had come through to her?' Blades said. 'Had it?'

Duggan shrugged his shoulders in a gesture that looked false to Blades. Then Duggan repeated it. 'If it had, she didn't tell me.'

'Would you expect her to be open about things like that?' Peacock said.

'She could be. She was a funny sort. She'd believe anything you said if it was romantic and the sort of thing she wanted to think about you. Like if I told her I was a hero in the war, or my family was descended from the aristocracy, it made her feel good about herself to think she'd attracted a catch like that. And she'd talk non-stop about the things she wanted out of life. And she had her dreams, that one. The moving pictures have a lot to answer for. She'd have loved to travel, see Europe and sail to America. She's not been out of Birtleby much that I know of. And she could clam up about herself if she wanted. Didn't want to put me off I suppose. Or maybe she didn't trust me enough.'

'Caught you out on one or two of your stories, then?' Peacock said.

'When she did that, she just talked herself into believing them again.'

'Someone ripe to be taken in by a rogue like you?' Peacock said.

'She was a person who could be taken in, but it wasn't by me. That's what I'm telling you. Look at Russell Parkes.'

'I see.' Blades gave Duggan some thought. 'Thank you for coming forward with this,' he said. 'Is there anything else you can tell us?'

'Not off-hand. But, I repeat, I would look at Russell Parkes.'

'Thank you, sir.'

Then Duggan left, and Blades tried to digest what he had just been told.

'It's a bit garbled and muddled,' Peacock said.

'Does that suggest it's true?'

'Only if Russell Parkes wasn't thinking straight when he did the murder – if he's the one who did it.'

'Opens up that line of inquiry again properly though. We've Russell to question about this – and his bookie.' Blades was pondering it all though. He was irritated by this. It wasn't as if they had been questioning Duggan. He had just turned up and provided more ammunition against Russell Parkes. How suspicious was that?

'Duggan always was questionable,' Blades said. 'Either he has difficulty thinking straight, or he's right about Russell Parkes, who does have a track record for violence.'

'If Parkes doesn't get his own way, he strikes out. Maybe he wasn't going to get the money he wanted from Emma, lashed out and killed her.'

'He wouldn't be able to get it from her if she didn't have it yet,' Blades repeated.

'We need to talk to the solicitors working on that estate as well.'

Blades paid no attention to that as his mind was elsewhere. 'Russell Parkes,' he said thoughtfully. 'We'll have to interview him.'

Blades reached for his coat and Peacock stood up ready to grasp his. Then the door opened and Moffat strode in, which surprised Blades. He sometimes wondered if Moffat just didn't have the energy to travel as far as this office. He always summoned Blades. Yet here he was, as self-righteous and uptight as ever, looking around him as if disliking everything he saw.

'Good morning, sir,' Blades said, giving Moffat his most affable smile.

CHAPTER THIRTY

'I want you to lay off Russell Parkes,' Moffat said.

'Really?' Blades and Peacock said almost in chorus. Everyone had been taking pains to point them at Parkes, Musgrave and Duggan at least, Blades was in the process of taking him seriously as a suspect, and now Moffat was placing him off limits.

'We haven't seen him in a while, sir,' Blades said, neglecting to say they had just been about to look him up. 'What makes you say that?'

'He has turned up in your investigations,' Moffat replied.

'As have others,' Blades replied.

'Yes, but Parkes is a dead end.'

Blades stared at Moffat. He had come over specially to say that? What was happening here?

'He has an uncle on the police board.'

'He does?'

'And he has expressed concern.'

'Should that make any difference?'

'If you value your job and I value mine, yes.'

'I can't believe you're saying that, sir. No one has impunity to commit murder.'

'No, but Russell Parkes hasn't committed any crime. I've spoken to his uncle and he's vouched for him. He's known the lad since he was knee-high, and he's never exhibited any nasty streak whatsoever. In fact, he's a young man who showed quite an interest in religion at one time. His family had hoped he might go in for the ministry. And he volunteers for charity work at his church regularly. He has quite the wrong character to be mixed up in anything like this. You're barking up the wrong tree, it's going to get you nowhere, and will have embarrassing political consequences. So, leave him alone.'

Blades had often wondered how someone like Moffat had become a Chief Constable. He had never noticed any real instinct for police work, a feeling for finance, possibly, but not the nitty-gritty of winkling out truths and villains. Perhaps he had advanced through managing not to offend anybody, something officers whose interest was in solving crimes couldn't help doing.

'The history of the courts throws up a lot of examples of apparently well-meaning people with lofty moral ambitions who have gone wrong – and committed extremely serious crimes,' Blades replied.

'Not Russell Parkes. The boy is innocent.'

'He has a police record,' Peacock said.

'Which involves violence against a woman,' Blades said.

'Only under great duress and provocation. You ought to study that case in greater depth than you have before commenting on it.'

Blades and Peacock had now fallen into silence. Blades did not know what to make of this visit from Moffat. The only conclusion he could come to was that behind that impressive exterior of Moffat's lay a surprisingly weak man.

'The search for the body,' Moffat said. 'How does that progress?'

The search Blades had been forced to ignore while he concentrated on other things, like Russell Parkes – and the

Roots – at Moffat's behest. Blades cursed inwardly. He had been hoping to liaise with the officers in charge of the search again. His lack of control of his own investigation was frustrating him.

'The search is still unproductive.' He did know that, unless something had turned up in the last hour or so.

'Which means you're pursuing what sort of case?' Moffat asked.

'Murder?' Blades replied. 'And we know it was Emma who was killed.'

'She's a missing person. That's all you have.'

'Considering what we found in the bath in the Roots' house–'

'You've formed an assumption. It does look as if someone has been seriously wounded but you don't know who and you have no body, which means you have no means of proving murder against anybody. Unless something approaching tangible evidence turns up about a murder and about the person who might have committed it, you're conducting an investigation on a scale and at an expense that's difficult to justify. And it's not just you who has to defend it. I have to do that too.'

'I beg to disagree,' Blades said. 'Emma Simpson has been murdered in that house, and, if we keep on searching for proof, we'll find it.'

'Have you made any further inquiries into Thomas Root?'

At least Blades did have a reply to that one.

'We interviewed him, sir, but couldn't elicit anything incriminating.'

'At least you've got round to talking to him again. I thought you were never going to follow up on that angle. Who are you going to interview next?'

'We'd thought of Russell Parkes but you've just told us to lay off him.'

'Which leaves Duggan, and you say you've nothing on him?'

'We haven't. No.'

'So, this is winding down. As far as the search is concerned, you have two more days to spend on that, and then it's called off, and you can concentrate on other cases, ones where there's a chance of securing a conviction against someone for something tangible. Now, overtime and holiday allowances, have you prepared the figures there for me to look at, yet? I've been asking you for those.'

Blades gave Moffat what he supposed was a weary look.

'You've been wasting your time chasing rainbows instead. Paperwork, paperwork, paperwork. That can't be emphasised enough. The fundamentals of administration are the building blocks of efficient policework, and you're always behind with yours.'

Blades supposed that was why they had to spend too much time in the office and not enough out questioning people, but all he said was, 'Yes, sir,' as he stood and tried not to look sullen. Peacock, he noticed, was inscrutable, though Peacock never looked like that unless he was furious.

After Moffat strode out just as grandly as he had arrived, Blades uttered an expression his wife would have been critical of. Then Peacock said, 'The speed he's closing this case down, you'd think Moffat had done it.'

'You might wonder,' Blades said, then muttered something else to himself before saying, 'but we've police work to do, and we'd better get on with it.'

'Reports?' Peacock said.

Blades grunted. 'No,' he said. 'It's time we interviewed Russell Parkes again.'

'Do you think that's wise?'

'No, but I say it has to be done.'

Blades reached for his cigarette packet, changed his mind, strode to the window and stared out. After some time, he returned his gaze to Peacock.

'In my entire police career, I've never been told something like that,' Blades said.

'It was surprising,' Peacock said. 'Somebody must have a lot of belief in Russell Parkes.'

'Unless they know he did it and don't want him caught.'

'An uncle might think like that.'

'I suppose a convicted murderer would spoil the family's reputation.'

'So, if we accept that's a possibility, what do we do about it?'

'Toe the line and keep our jobs?' Blades suggested.

'Get some paperwork done?'

Then Blades gave a bitter laugh. 'I don't know how we can go on to anything else without questioning Parkes first.'

He noticed the suggestion of a grin appearing around Peacock's mouth, which echoed his own feelings.

CHAPTER THIRTY-ONE

The interview room in Birtleby Police Station was not only bare but bleak, with its uncared-for walls direly in need of a splash of paint, its worn flooring, and the charming view from its window of a brick wall. When Blades and Peacock had caught up with Parkes, he'd been leaving the house of a customer and was indignant to find he was being taken in for questioning. He mentioned his uncle's name several times in the police car on the way to the station, but Blades and Peacock paid no attention to this, so now Russell was squirming on a wooden seat opposite them.

'You're right,' Blades said. 'It has been suggested we dismiss you from the case.'

Parkes gave Blades a puzzled look.

'So?'

'So,' Blades replied, 'that's what we're doing. We're giving you a chance to clear yourself once and for all. I suggest that you take it.'

Parkes slumped in the seat with a sullen expression; his eyes threatened dreadful things to Blades.

'You knew Emma,' Blades said, 'though at first you denied knowing her as well as you did. You were good friends with her, weren't you?'

Russell obviously resented the question, but he did reply, 'She was a pleasant enough girl. She played a good instrument too.'

'You've at no time expressed sorrow over her disappearance or death.'

Russell's eyes bored into Blades again. 'What's that supposed to mean?'

'You haven't, have you?'

'It was a bit of a shock,' Russell said. 'I didn't know what to say. That ought to be plain to see. It's a dreadful thing that a young woman like her has had her life taken from her. Obviously, I feel for her.'

'It hasn't been clear to us that you do,' Peacock said. 'This is the first time you've expressed any feelings about her at all.'

'Then I was remiss and I'm sorry.' Russell gave them both a beaming smile. 'So, can I go now?' he said.

Peacock's look was withering, and Blades hoped his was the same. 'You've lied to us,' he said.

'You were trying to pin something on me,' Parkes replied.

'You knew her, and we were asking you questions,' Blades replied, 'to which you gave untrue answers. Lucky you, having an uncle to stick up for you.'

'All right. I'm sorry about that too.' The tone was almost flippant, Blades thought, as if Russell assumed they had no power here. Arrogance like that did not suggest innocence to Blades.

'First, you swore you knew Emma less well than you did, and then you fabricated an alibi.'

'An alibi? Oh, that?'

'Rose was working on the Saturday when you said you were with her. She does agree she was with you on the Friday and went walking in the park with you then and listened to the band.'

Parkes shrugged both shoulders in an exaggerated way.

'I got mixed up about the day, all right?'

'So, what were you doing on the Saturday of Emma's disappearance?' Blades asked.

'Damned if I can remember,' Russell replied, and the insolence was provocative.

'That's a pity,' Peacock said. 'Have you any idea how suspicious that looks?'

'I'll have to think about what I was up to,' Russell said, but did not elaborate.

'No alibi?' Blades said.

Russell was staring back in silence now.

'And about your previous conviction,' Blades said, 'what were the extenuating circumstances I've been told existed?'

Russell's immediate reply was a glare, but then he thought better of it. 'She volunteered the money and then didn't turn up with it. I was a bit exasperated.'

'More than that. You broke her cheekbone.'

Now there was a genuine reaction from Russell, and he was annoyed again. 'No. I did not. She fell and broke her cheekbone.'

'After you'd struck her.'

'After I swung my arm back, but I didn't bring it forward. I didn't intend to hit her. It was only a threat. But she jumped back and then fell over.'

'Really?'

'Really.'

'So, why didn't the court believe you at the time?'

'The jury took to her more than me.'

Was that believable, Blades wondered. The answer came back no. 'So, when you're in debt again,' he said, 'something happens to another young lady you know. That's a coincidence. As is the fact you have miraculously managed to pay off your gambling debts just when your bookie was threatening to break both of your legs.'

There was surprise in Russell's eyes now – he had not expected Blades to know that – but that, too, turned to annoyance.

'I admit it looks bad,' he said.

'Doesn't it?' Peacock said.

'But it isn't what it looks like.'

'So, what is it?' Peacock asked.

'You can win when you gamble as well. That's the whole point of gambling. And I did.'

'So, a bookie can vouch for this?' Blades said. 'That's good. What's his name?'

'It was a lot of small bets with different bookies at the turf. On the same horse. I have debts. I had to spread the bet around.'

'What you're saying is that it can't be verified.'

Russell shrugged his perennially expressive shoulders. 'You can ask around. Individually, the wins were small. Some of them might remember, I suppose.'

'We know about Emma's inheritance.'

'That's more than I do. Was she going to come into money? Who from?'

Blades looked at the expression on Parkes' face, and it did not look truthful.

'You've no alibi,' Blades repeated, 'and I doubt if you've given an honest answer to anything you've been asked.'

'You've no proof I did anything to Emma. Come out with it if you have. Go on. What evidence do you have against me?'

Blades could only stare back at him and seethe. When he did speak, the words came out with reluctance. 'Which is true,' he said. 'So, all right, Mr Parkes, unless some turns up and gives me another reason for questioning you, I'll leave you in peace.'

'Until it does,' Peacock added.

And if it did not, Blades knew that he would have to stay away from him, but at least he had satisfied his curiosity and knew exactly where they were with the precious Russell Parkes.

CHAPTER THIRTY-TWO

'I was a friend of Emma's,' the young woman seated in front of Blades and Peacock said. 'And my name is Harriet Haigh.'

Blades was wondering how Peacock had found her. She was exactly what he had been hoping to find, someone who could give them some sort of insight into their victim. Emma was still too much of a mystery for Blades. There was something about her he had not grasped; in fact, he was sure there was a lot.

Blades studied Harriet. She was a pale, thin young woman with a subdued look. He supposed it might be because of where she was.

'I'm a seamstress,' she said, 'and I knew Emma. Our families lived just up the street from each other at one point.'

'And you still knew her?' Blades asked.

'Oh, yes. We used to meet up at Lyons now and again. It's good to get away from work and have a tea and a chat with someone.'

'So, is there anything you can tell us that might help us with her disappearance?'

'I don't know, but I can tell you more about Emma.'

'Did she have plans to go away anywhere?'

'She didn't talk about them with me and I'm sure she would have done. She probably would have loved the chance to go away somewhere else for a break at least. Wouldn't we all? It's hard enough getting from one day to the next, isn't it?'

'Tell me about it,' Blades said. And he gave her a smile as if to suggest he shared her experience of the world and the weariness of it.

'So, what did Emma talk about?' he asked.

'Anything and everything. She was chatty and she was good for a laugh. She was fun to be with.'

'So, nothing was worrying her?'

'She didn't like Thomas Root.'

'She didn't?'

'Hands everywhere. She had to fend him off. Only the once, mind, but that's too often, isn't it? She stopped laughing at his jokes and being friendly after that.'

'Did his wife know?'

'She wasn't supposed to, but she must have done. It's not exactly a big place. Anyway, that's what Emma threatened him with, that she'd tell her. It worked. The only thing is he turned his attentions to that daily maid Louisa instead. She's no better than she ought to be. Emma said Louisa enjoyed it. She encouraged him. I thought that was probably a good thing, but Emma worried for Louisa then. She would. That's the sort Emma was. I often told her she cared too much about things. She ought to be just glad Louisa was distracting Thomas from her.'

'That's just the sort she was,' Blades said. 'What do you mean by that?'

'Emma was proper. She thought things ought to be as they should. She'd a real sense of right and wrong. I remember her telling me about school, when a boy was being punished for something he hadn't done. I don't remember what it was. Oh, yes, I do. Someone had put glue on the teacher's chair, and this boy Douglas was the one who got the blame. I don't know why. He always was in trouble about one thing or another.'

'But it wasn't him this time?' Peacock asked.

'It was a great lump called Fred. And he'd done it to get Douglas into trouble. He owed him one because he'd told on him one time.'

'And Emma didn't think that was right.'

'No, she didn't. But she knew she would never get Fred to admit to it. Do you know what she did? She admitted to doing it herself.'

'She did?' Blades said. 'That was brave.'

'She took the cane for someone else.'

'And what did Douglas do?'

'He wasn't worth the effort. He just smirked off. Thought if she was stupid enough to admit to it, fair enough. Only thing he knew was he hadn't done it.'

'Interesting,' Blade said.

'So, why are you telling us this?' Peacock asked.

'She didn't think it was right the way Mr Root was treating Louisa. She faced Louisa with it, and they had a dreadful row. She told Louisa it wasn't right, and Louisa turned around and stuck up for him. I don't know why Emma was bothering trying to help her. I don't think Louisa minded Mr Root nipping her bottom now and again.'

'Had Emma decided to do something about it?' Blades asked. 'What?'

'She knew she wouldn't get any joy from Mr Root. She said she would tell Mrs Root. I told her she probably knew already, so what good would that do? Emma said Mrs Root couldn't know, and, if she did, she couldn't like it and needed to be encouraged to sort her husband out.'

'Did she say when she was going to talk to Mrs Root about this?' Peacock asked.

'Friday.'

'That's Friday the fourteenth?' Blades asked. 'Just before she disappeared?'

'I don't know exactly when that was.'

'She was last seen on Saturday, the fifteenth,' Blades replied.

That struck Harriet. She went quiet for a minute and Blades could swear her skin turned paler.

'The day before she disappeared. Do you suppose that had anything to do with it?'

'It's a line of inquiry,' Blades said.

'Definitely suspicious,' Peacock said.

'Isn't it?' Harriet said, and her eyes were wide.

'Did she tell you what she was going to say to Mrs Root?' Blades asked.

'She was going to tell her Mr Root was carrying on with Louisa and that Mrs Root ought to put a stop to it before it led to anything. Louisa was a young girl and needed protecting.'

'That's straightforward enough,' Blades said.

'And Amelia ought to remember all about that,' Peacock said.

'I wonder what that led to?' Blades said. This was something to question Amelia Root about – and Thomas.

All three of them sat for a moment lost in thought, and the silence felt overwhelming to Blades.

CHAPTER THIRTY-THREE

Amelia's dignified pose had slipped.

'You're saying my husband has been bothering Louisa?'

Blades and Peacock were seated with Amelia in her parlour. Amelia was slightly crumpled in her seat as if having difficulty in coping with the statement she had just heard. Both men were upright and alert in theirs. The disbelief in Amelia's eyes was convincing, Blades thought. Anyone would have thought any suggestion of misbehaviour between Thomas and Louisa was news to Amelia.

'Emma told you about this before she disappeared.'

An irritated look had now appeared on Amelia's face. 'Thomas wouldn't behave like that. He has a position in the town.'

And that was less convincing. Was Amelia really saying the only reason Thomas wouldn't bother Louisa was that it would affect his standing with the neighbours? Was this how a wife reacted when she heard her husband was straying?

'And he's related to her. It would be unthinkable.'

Why was there no suggestion Thomas loved Amelia too much to do such a thing? Blades glanced across at

Peacock, and took in the doubting look on his face, before turning his gaze on Amelia again.

'It's surprising how often I come across that sort of thing, as a police officer,' Blades said. 'I can find it difficult to believe a husband hasn't strayed.'

A snort erupted from the haughty Amelia; she opened her mouth to speak but closed it again. Her mind was racing, with what thoughts was what Blades was trying to work out.

'I don't know what you mean,' she said.

'Louisa's an attractive young lady,' Peacock said. 'Vivacious, lively, and at an age when she might be expected to be tempted by a bit of fun. Was Thomas?'

'Definitely not,' Amelia said.

'How can you be sure?' Peacock asked.

'I know my husband,' Amelia said.

'It was worrying Emma,' Blades said.

'What was?' Amelia asked, and her voice had risen.

'Emma came across the pair of them having a cuddle,' Peacock said.

'She felt concerned for Louisa,' Blades added. 'She taxed Louisa with it and told her she would talk to Thomas – and tell you if it continued.'

'I know nothing about this,' Amelia said.

'She was threatening to speak to you on the Friday before you left on your holiday.'

'The day before she disappeared,' Peacock added.

Amelia stared from one of them to the other, but said nothing, and seemed at a loss.

'Did she tell you what your husband was up to?' Blades asked.

'Definitely not. Are you suggesting Thomas did away with Emma because of that?' she asked.

'Is he the kind of man who would do that?' Blades asked.

'Definitely not,' Amelia replied. But that was all she said. It did strike Blades she was hiding something, though he could not work out what. Blades thought Amelia had probably known for some time Thomas was misbehaving, but he wondered how she might have reacted when Emma faced her with it.

Amelia was now upright and the expression on her face was one of indignation and anger, as she struggled to assert herself. 'I must ask you to apologise for insinuations about Thomas. He's never strayed; he's not the type of man to do that and certainly not with the likes of Louisa. Louisa was common, even if she was Thomas's second cousin. He was fond of her – they were related – but Emma was mistaken if she thought there was something going on between him and Louisa. And he wouldn't be violent towards Emma. I've been married to him for thirty years, and he's never lifted a finger to me. He's not an aggressive man.'

'So, Emma talked about this with Thomas?' Blades said.

As Amelia gazed back at him, Blades could see another emotion working its way through her. Along with the anger, there was what looked like shame.

'All right,' Amelia said. 'And she brought it up with me as well. But Emma was wrong. I can see Louisa setting her cap at a man, but the idea that Thomas would respond to this' – and here Amelia struggled for words – 'is ridiculous.'

The glare Blades received from Amelia had the self-righteousness and resentment in it he would expect, but also something Amelia might not have realised was obvious – doubt.

With a tolerant look on his face, Peacock said, 'Men can find things difficult at a certain age.'

'Not my Thomas.'

'We've agreed Emma did raise suspicions with your husband about what was going on between him and Louisa,' Blades said.

Blades winced at the venom that appeared on Amelia's face, but she did not say any more.

'What was Thomas's reaction to this?' he asked, then waited for a reply, but none came. 'And how could Emma be wrong about something like that?'

'Maybe she misinterpreted something that she saw.'

'That sounds difficult.'

Amelia stood up and put on a most dignified expression. 'This interview is at an end,' she said.

But when Blades told her to sit down again, she did.

'There must have been strong emotions around on the day you set off on holiday,' Blades said. 'You were angry, probably with your husband, and definitely with Emma. Thomas would have been furious at being found out; Emma would be indignant. All that must have led to a serious argument.'

'Did you strike out at Emma?' Peacock said.

'I most certainly did not.'

Then Amelia burst into tears, and Blades wondered if this was the last weapon in her armoury. They had her backed into a corner but all they could do was watch her weep. And she still wasn't telling them what they wanted to know.

CHAPTER THIRTY-FOUR

'What's this you've been upsetting Amelia about?' Thomas Root's voice was indignant, his expression authoritative.

Blades glowered in return, as did Peacock.

Thomas had burst in on their interview. As it was taking place in Thomas's own parlour, he could not be refused entry. Perhaps Amelia's sobs had been intended as a cry to him.

'It's my job to ask questions,' Blades replied.

'And the questions are simple,' Peacock said. 'It's answers that can be difficult.'

Before Thomas had the chance to shout as his expression suggested he was about to do, Blades exerted his own authority. He might as well put pressure on Thomas too, as he was there. 'We know you were having a flirtation with Louisa, Emma had found out about this, and decided to face both you and your wife with it.'

Thomas's mouth had been open, ready to speak, but he shut it. When he did speak, all he said was, 'Do you?'

'It must have been an awkward scene.'

'Is that when you struck out at Emma and killed her?' Peacock asked.

Thomas considered his options before speaking.

'Strike her? I didn't do that. I don't know how she died, if she did, or why she disappeared. That has nothing to do with me.'

'It was quite an argument between the three of you,' Blades said. 'And just before Emma disappeared. A coincidence, wouldn't you say?'

'All right, all right,' Thomas replied, and there was a look of defeat on his face. 'There was an argument. You're right about that – and that's it.'

Amelia had stopped sobbing immediately when Thomas appeared. There was consternation on her face now, as if she could not work out what ploy to try next. Blades gave her a commanding look. 'Mrs Root, we would like to talk to Thomas on his own now.'

Amelia looked questioningly at Thomas.

'It's all right,' he said to her. Then, after a pause while she seemed to be working out whether to do this or not, she departed, with a baffled expression on her face, but also some relief.

Blades turned back to Thomas. 'So, tell us about it,' he said.

The anger had left Thomas's face.

'Louisa?' he replied.

'That's correct,' Blades said.

Then, with reluctance, Thomas started to answer the question. 'I'd been having a bit of fun,' Thomas said. 'That's all.' Then he stopped.

'Go on,' Blades said.

'It wasn't supposed to lead to anything,' Thomas replied. 'Really.' And his eyes appealed to be believed. 'A flirtation. You don't know Louisa the way I do. If you did, you would realise it was, as it were, passing the time. Harmless.' Then Thomas stopped talking and Blades had the impression he could not believe what he had said.

'She didn't matter, in other words?' Peacock said.

Thomas glared at Peacock before replying. 'That's not what I meant. You don't get it. She was up for it. She started it. She harassed me.'

'I see,' Blades said, not that he did.

Thomas looked from one to the other as if looking for help somewhere. 'Really,' he said. 'I mean. You're men. You understand.'

But all they did was look back.

'Don't you? Well, you should. It was joking about. That was all.'

'And did your wife agree with that when Emma told her?' Peacock asked.

Thomas ignored that. 'You know what women are like,' Thomas said, looking at Blades. 'Of course she didn't. She was livid. I could have killed Emma.' Then Thomas stopped, as he realised what he had just said.

'And did you?' Blades asked.

'I mean. I don't mean – oh, it's an expression. That's all. Of course, I didn't.'

'So, where is she, sir?' Blades asked.

'I don't know,' Thomas replied, and he spread his arms wide. 'I don't know,' he repeated. And he looked from one to the other, before again saying, 'I don't know. I tell you. I don't.'

'Did Amelia strike Emma?' Blades asked.

'Of course she didn't.'

'She could have struck out,' Peacock said, 'just meaning to give her a bit of a slap.'

'Or you could,' Blades said.

'Just to make her stop talking, that was all,' Peacock added.

'Only it went further than that – somehow, didn't it?' Blades said.

'No. No. It wasn't like that.'

'So, tell us what it was like,' Blades said.

'We just argued. I had to explain myself to Amelia. It was embarrassing. And Amelia was furious. She fairly lashed at me with her tongue, I can tell you. I'll have to behave myself in future.'

'So, she was grateful to Emma for telling her,' Peacock said.

'She wasn't grateful for anything at the time. I'll swear she had no idea before then. That Emma. What she was getting up to with that Alfred Duggan, and she has the nerve to rat on me. And it was about nothing.'

'You were angry with Emma?' Blades said.

Root retreated into silence again for a moment or two as he grappled with that question.

'Of course, I was angry with her, but I don't suppose I should have been flirting with Louisa in the first place. That wasn't something I would take out on Emma.'

'When you've time to think about it, you see that,' Blades said, 'but in the heat of the moment?'

'No. No. No. I didn't do anything to Emma, I tell you.'

And Thomas Root was now completely backed into a corner, and Blades could tell he was not going to get past those denials, but he would continue questioning him.

'How long did the argument last?'

Thomas thought about that. 'That's difficult to say. Half an hour, I suppose, to talk it through with Emma. Fending off Amelia's accusations took at least the rest of the day.'

'When did you leave Birtleby?'

'We were supposed to leave at ten.'

'In your statement that was when you said you left.'

'Was it? And we would have done if–' Thomas now had to think things through again. 'Well, it held us up. I don't know. I didn't look at the clock. We might have left – when? – about eleven, maybe after that.'

'So, the argument must have lasted about an hour?' Blades said.

A defeated look was on Thomas's face again.

'If you say so.'

'It still doesn't take six hours to travel to Ramshead from Birtleby.'

'I told you what we were doing in that time.'

'Were you disposing of a body? Were you cleaning up at the house to hide traces of a scuffle and a murder?' Blades asked.

'Of course not,' Thomas said. 'And you can't prove that either.'

'Not at the moment,' Blades said. 'But we will need a new statement from you, and from Amelia.'

'I liked Emma,' Thomas said. 'She was a good sort. A bit of a goody-goody-two-shoes, and not half judgemental when she felt like it. But she was young. What do you expect? No experience of the world. She was a well-meaning sort. Not that she needed to worry about Louisa. But I could see why she might. And Emma wasn't half a good worker. And she had a good way with the customers. And everybody. I liked the girl. I wouldn't kill her. And neither would Amelia.'

Blades forced patience on himself. He had heard denials like these before, but, if he could turn up some vestige of proof, then he might force a confession out of Thomas – or even Amelia. He had not dismissed her either.

CHAPTER THIRTY-FIVE

As the search for the missing body had continued in Birtleby, the sky had turned into a mass of brooding clouds that unleashed rain with what felt like venom; drains overloaded, with pools of water stretching out from them; and water ran in rivers from gutters on roofs, all of which made the work increasingly arduous. Boots tramped through muddy puddles, rain dripped from helmets and found its way past coat collars, but constables still probed into back yards and through middens.

For the moment, Blades was standing in his office with Peacock beside him, staring out at the weather.

'That'll play havoc with any evidence they come across,' he said.

'It won't melt parts of a body,' Peacock replied.

'It'll destroy any other traces they might find beside them.'

'We might not need anything else.'

Blades just grunted in reply to that.

Searches were still ongoing between Birtleby and Ramshead as well. Hopes had been raised by some bones, but they had turned out to be animal. Constables had been drafted in from other areas; overtime rotas had been plundered; money had been borrowed from other budgets, and Blades could quite see why Moffat wanted a result or an end to all of this. The searchers' patience was being stretched, and tempers were fraying as eyes peered, and sticks overturned. On top of everything else, newspaper reporters had started to turn up in unprecedented droves.

The rain continued to thunder down as the weather and the mood became gloomier. Then something was found, and Blades and Peacock were called out to inspect it.

It had been discovered in a midden between two rows of workers' terraced cottages. Rubbish was brought here before being collected by town trucks. The place was a tumble of bags and bins, the detritus of everyday. Like any such collection of unwanted things it had a random feel to it, as if everything was only here by accident, but there was now an area that had been purposefully marked off, and was being guarded by not one but two constables still with rain dripping from helmets and capes. Peacock had his camera out and ready. Blades' eyes peered ahead of him eagerly. He came level with the first constable.

'So, where is it?'

The constable pointed directly behind him.

Blades found himself looking at a pile of empty tins.

'Is this it?'

'Over there,' the constable said, pointing again.

And Blades saw it. There was a recognizable pattern to that arrangement of bones and torn flesh, and it was human; it was a hand.

Blades muttered. Peacock swore. Both of them stared.

'Could be a woman's hand,' Blades said.

'Or a child's?'

'I hope not,' Blades said. 'That would mean another victim.'

'The pathologist will tell us.'

Blades' eyes searched all around the midden.

'I suppose this has all been sifted through,' Blades said to the constable.

'Yes, sir.'

'Did you find clothing, or anything else that might suggest a connection with this?'

The constable shook his head.

'It'll all have to be sifted through again.'

Oh yes, Blades thought. They would peer for anything else that might give a clue to the identity of the owner of the hand, or the identity of the person who had left it there. Peacock started taking his photographs of the hand in situ, then the greater scene, while Blades pondered his calmness. Peacock was looking at a human hand, unattached to anything, with total professional detachment, when all Blades could feel was horror.

Had the murderer taken the time and trouble to scatter Emma around in various places, a piece at a time? Why? To make it more difficult to find the body, or identify it? If he had completed the task in different places, it ought to make it easier to find someone who had seen him. The killer would have worked that out. Unless he had dumped Emma in one spot, and this hand had been dragged about by some animal. Blades glared at it. They would bag it, have it studied in a lab, and find out as much as they could from it. Blades pondered his assumption that the culprit was a 'he'. Then he returned to the idea this body part had been brought here by an animal. That would mean the rest of Emma could be somewhere in this general area. Blades would make sure efforts were redoubled.

He became aware of how dark his mood was. This was a triumph, more proof of murder as insisted on by Moffat, and he ought to have been cheerful, but he was still looking at a dismembered hand.

It was then that he noticed the break in the clouds above Birtleby. There was a patch of sky that was lighter just over there. Blades could only hope that held meaning.

CHAPTER THIRTY-SIX

The report on the hand had come in. Blades and Peacock had both read it by now and Peacock was standing by Blades' desk so they could discuss it.

'Moffat can't drop the inquiry now,' Peacock said.

'It's definitely murder,' Blades said. 'And, at some point, we'll turn up the rest of that body.'

'And then we'll know who the murderer is?'

'Have we dismissed any suspects?'

'Not that Duggan.'

'And the Roots look increasingly shifty.'

'And there's Russell Parkes.'

'Whom we've to steer clear of,' Blades said, 'which we can do, though it won't stop us investigating, and if we find proof Russell did this, Moffat can take a running jump.'

Blades looked at the report again and frowned.

'Definitely the hand of a female of Emma's age. About a week since death is the estimate, which fits in with the time of her disappearance. There are marks that suggest an animal has been at the hand. It's probably been taken from a pile of other parts, which means the rest shouldn't be far off even if no one has turned them up yet.' Blades frowned again. 'So, you're definitely dead, Emma,' he said, and there was a heaviness in his voice.

'We knew that,' Peacock said.

'We could have hoped we were wrong,' Blades said. 'We can't now.'

He continued to look at the report, then pushed it away from him. He took out a Woodbine and lit it. It was something to do while he thought, not that thinking was getting him anywhere. 'There's nothing resembling proof against Russell Parkes. We've no more against Duggan, and what we have is insufficient. And there's certainly not enough against the Roots.'

'Perhaps Musgrave will turn up with more information against someone.'

'There's a cheerful thought,' Blades said, and a thoughtful look came over his face. 'Or Duggan might,' he said. 'Duggan came forward twice with information against Parkes.'

'And took the chance to ask questions about the course of the investigation.'

'When someone is being as helpful and inquisitive as that, you do wonder. Is he our culprit?'

'It has been known,' Peacock said.

'There was the Higgins case in London,' Blades replied. 'A young woman killed, Higgins a caring teacher and friend who went out of his way to help with the inquiry – or steer it away from himself if he could. It turned out that not only had he murdered that young woman but there was another in his spare bedroom he'd killed since then.'

'I remember that one,' Peacock said.

'What do we really know about Duggan?'

'Don't we know quite a lot? They must have investigated him pretty thoroughly before charging him with bigamy.'

Blades reached to the shelf above him for a file and took it down. He leafed through several pages, then muttered to himself. He straightened up and leaned back in his chair. Looking directly at Peacock, he asked him, 'What did you really make of him in those interviews?'

Peacock gave this some thought. 'Untrustworthy?'

'Did he come across as a bit irrational?'

'I don't think so. Was he?'

'If he's come forward with information to distract us, how stupid does he think we are?'

'A lot of people underestimate the police, criminals anyway.'

'He started off by saying he hadn't seen Emma for three weeks before she disappeared, then came forward and admitted he'd seen her just the day before, without any pressure from us. I'm trying to follow the reasoning there.'

'He knew we were asking around and would probably find out?'

'Maybe. Then he was the one who came forward with information Russell Parkes had been seeing Emma.'

'Musgrave did as well.'

'Where did Musgrave get his information from?' Blades asked. 'He wouldn't say. But they were both right. Parkes was seeing Emma.'

'And they both suggested a motive for Parkes. Parkes had gambling debts.'

'And Duggan said Emma was coming into money. Did we ever get that inheritance confirmed?' Blades said.

'Good point.'

'Not that it made any sense even if Emma was coming into money. She didn't have it yet. What benefit is that to Parkes? Either Parkes is muddled in his thinking or Duggan is. And bigamy. That's a funny game, and difficult not to get caught out on it. How sensibly did Duggan go about that?' Blades leafed through the papers in front of him again. 'Not very. Second wife not at the other end of the country – in the next town, which was only a few miles away.'

'Not the most intelligent of men?'

A thought occurred to Blades. 'What was Duggan's war record?' He leafed through the papers again. 'It's not mentioned here.'

'Did he fight?'

'Was he wounded? Shellshock? What was he like before the war? Was he anything like he was after it?'

'They're good questions, sir.'

'Or not. Perhaps he's just annoyed me. I don't like having my inquiries being led by someone else.'

'Musgrave was suggesting the same things Duggan was.'

Blades' look was dismissive.

'He's a journalist. He's looking for stories. I doubt if he even cares if they're true, just believable. But Duggan, what does go on there?'

'Musgrave will have a better story to write now that hand has turned up.'

'That's a point,' Blades said. 'I'll have to give thought to the press release.'

But his mind was not on it yet. He reached for his Woodbines. It might take a whole packet to work out everything his mind was working on. He muttered. 'After that conversation with the Roots,' he said, 'I was convinced Thomas did it.'

'You think?' Peacock asked.

'Or not.'

Blades was aware of the disconsolate look there must be on his face but he did nothing to dismiss it, just lit the cigarette.

CHAPTER THIRTY-SEVEN

When Blades came out of the police station, he was surrounded by a flash of camera bulbs, a flurry of reporters with notebooks and pencils raised, and a storm of discordant voices.

'What can you tell us about the latest developments?'

'How close are you to announcing an arrest?'

'Do you have a confession?'

'Have you proved it's murder yet?'

'Is it true Emma's been found alive?'

Blades took a step back as he tried to take all of this in. He was surrounded by the faces of journalists of differing ages and body types. There were some who would never see fifty again, and others who looked as if they might not have started shaving yet. Some looked anything but physically fit, being rotund in body shape and sounding short in breath. Blades had often wondered at the lifestyle of reporters. He supposed they found themselves at desks a lot, and, at other times, in search of stories in the unhealthy environments of pubs, and places of entertainment from the dubious to the edifying. They must spend a lot of time hanging around waiting for stories outside police stations, in hospitals, at mortuaries, and sniffing round various scenes of mayhem and accident. What came across most clearly to him from this lot was the contradictory nature of the questions. These reporters didn't even know whether it was murder, a missing persons case, or if Emma had returned. So, why the snap surge? As he scanned the crowd, he made out the face of Musgrave, and was glad to see him for the first time. He was familiar.

As Blades opened his mouth to speak, another camera bulb exploded next to his face and blinded him. He shook his head and waited for vision to return. Struggling to come to terms with all of this, he gave an automatic reaction. 'There have been no developments,' he said.

A voice shouted out, 'We've been told different. What's the breakthrough?'

'Breakthrough?' Blades said. 'You tell me. I wish we'd had one.'

'We know different,' shouted out another voice. 'Give.'

'Why the total silence?' another voice said. 'Readers are entitled to know.'

'Is it Root?' shouted another. 'We know you've been interviewing him.'

'And we know Duggan's been in the frame.'

'And Russell Parkes.'

'You've found the body? Is that it?' came another voice.

'Was it Emma Simpson's?' said another.

Blades supposed the only way to respond was to make use of the opportunity to bring them up to date. Though what was there to tell them? He and his men were still out there asking questions and wondering why they could not find answers. He was beating his head against a brick wall over and over again and the only thing he was discovering was that it hurt.

'I'll make a statement,' he said.

'About time,' was shouted out.

'Get started,' another voice blurted out.

Blades was not accustomed to this. The reporters they usually saw in Birtleby were not quite this demanding.

'We continue our search for a body,' he said. 'There's enough evidence in the Roots' house for us to assume death by foul play. We have interviewed everyone connected with Emma but have found no grounds to charge anyone as yet.'

'Why have you dropped any investigation into Russell Parkes?' a voice sang out.

'What?' Blades said. It was not the first time in this case that he had been surprised at the amount of knowledge held by a reporter, and this was particularly mystifying. There was no way Moffat had announced that publicly, he hadn't, and he did not believe Peacock would have done. So, where had that information come from?'

Another question was shot at Blades. 'Russell Parkes knew the victim and gave a false alibi for the time of her disappearance. Why isn't he still an official suspect?'

Blades glowered in the direction of the questioner but knew better than to speak in anger.

'No one has been officially pronounced a suspect or officially dismissed as one,' he said in as neutral a tone as he could summon. 'You mention Russell Parkes and I can confirm that he has been questioned, and, if further reasons to question him occur, he will be asked to co-operate with our inquiries again. But I wish to cast no slur upon anyone against whom we have no proof. When there are grounds to charge someone, that will be done.' Blades hoped that was a clever answer. With any luck it would appease both the journalist and Russell Parkes' uncle, and keep him on the right side of professionalism.

'Why are we being warned against asking Russell Parkes questions but not Alfred Duggan or Thomas Root?' the voice went on.

Why indeed, Blades thought, and who was doing the warning?

'I doubt if that's true.' He was sure it sounded lame as he said it.

'What's the latest development we've been told of?' another voice sounded out.

'I don't know who gave that information, but it wasn't on my instructions,' Blades said. 'But I can tell you that bodily remains have turned up in the search area, namely, a human hand – and that of a young woman of about Emma's age, but we've no evidence it belongs to Emma, though circumstances obviously suggest it.'

'That's what you've been keeping quiet about?' said a voice.

'That's a major development,' said another.

More camera bulbs flashed as questions rang out about the hand, not all of which Blades could decipher. In any case, what more details were there to give the press about that?

'We would like to appeal as usual for witnesses to help the investigation move further forward. If anyone saw Emma recently in the company of someone else, in particular someone male, could they please get in touch? And, if anyone heard or saw anything unusual in the Root household or in its vicinity on or around Saturday the fifteenth, we would very much like to hear from them.'

Then Blades turned to leave. He hoped he had appeased them. They had a headline and a story, and perhaps Blades could get back to his job in peace. Peacock had the Ford pulled up outside the police station and Blades opened the door and stepped into it. At least no one was shouting anything at him anymore and they had not followed him. Then a head appeared beside the car window. It was Musgrave. Blades thought he had been unusually quiet during the reporters' ruckus. What did Musgrave want?

'You know, don't you?' Musgrave said, and his voice was low, almost a whisper.

'Know what?' Blades said.

'A hundred yards away from where your search stopped, that's all.'

'What?'

'You had to finish somewhere, I know, but it wasn't that far from where you found the hand.'

Blades gave him a puzzled stare.

'The rest of her. She's all there.'

Blades opened his mouth, but no words came out. Even if that were true, how would Musgrave know about it?

'The copse by the railway bridge. She's in there.'

Then Musgrave turned and walked quickly away, leaving Blades staring after him. His investigation was being directed by someone else yet again, and if Musgrave was right, this was crucial.

CHAPTER THIRTY-EIGHT

It looked as much of a fly-tip as a copse to Blades, who was looking at a couple of discarded prams, half a bike, several indeterminate heaps of scrap metal, and countless tins, filthy rags, and scraps of newspaper, all tangled up with the long grass and bramble between the bedraggled birch trees. He and Peacock had gone straight to the area Musgrave had pointed them to. Musgrave had been right before, so Blades had brought constables with him, and he soon had them spread out, walking in as straight a line as they could manage, prodding with sticks.

It might not be raining but it was a grey day again, and Blades was in yet another depressed mood. What he was looking at was bad enough but what he hoped to find would be worse. He reflected again that it was the nature of his job that his triumphs were always tinged by the tragedy of the crime. Then a breeze blew up, sending a piece of newspaper flying. The air was cold to the skin, the light dull to the eye, and the ground squelched underfoot, evidence of the recent days of rain. Their investigation, like the weather, had penetrated the soul, and there was nothing to be done about that but trudge on and poke with his stick.

Their first find was an old case hidden under the brambles, which was difficult to haul out; it turned out to be empty, but Blades told Peacock to photograph it, and ordered a constable to carry it to the boot of the Ford. It might not yield anything but it ought to be examined. Had that been the find Musgrave had said with such certainty was waiting for them? If it was, Blades would have something to say to him. Blades and Peacock and the six constables trudged on, pulling at vegetation, and poking underneath. They worked in silence, each face a picture of concentration, as they made their progress forward. The undergrowth was thicker than Blades had realised, the copse larger, and the search was slow, but that did not deter them.

There was a shout from one of the constables, and Blades looked across at him. He was not a man Blades had much to do with before. He was a large-framed, cumbersome man with a saturnine face and Blades had no idea how reliable he was. The constable had overturned one of the prams which seemed to have been hiding something. Blades walked over to him, but saw nothing, just a heap of rags. He poked right through them with his stick but there was no sign of any flesh or bones, so there was no reason to suppose these rags had anything to do with the disappearance of Emma.

'No,' he said to the constable. 'Well spotted, though. Keep it up.'

Blades returned to where he had been searching. The slow tramp forward continued for some time. Occasionally, something was turned up requiring further study by one of the others, but these objects also proved to be nothing and were tossed to the side as the search continued. Blades was coming to the conclusion this was another wild goose chase, and was silently cursing, when his eyes did alight on something as he pulled back an old, torn tarpaulin. That he was the one to find this was luck, but it still felt like a personal triumph. His eyes were gazing greedily on not one but two large, leather suitcases, both of which matched a description given by a witness. One case was half open and Blades could already see what it contained. He held up his arm and yelled. 'Here. Over here.' Then Peacock was beside him and without needing to be told, was taking careful photographs from a myriad of different angles.

Wrapped in different, bloodstained paper parcels, like so much butcher's meat, was the flesh and bone of something, and, in the context, it was obvious these would be confirmed as human parts and, Blades was sure, the paltry remains of Emma Simpson. He poked at the grisly find, slowly, and with care. This would be etched in his memory, but that did not deter him. He hoped there would be clothing that could help identify the victim – or anything else that might do that. But he found nothing but blood, and flesh, and bone, and more blood.

He pushed that case to the side then had Peacock photograph the second case and dust it for prints as well, before he opened it, not that there would be any, he expected, after the rain there had been. Then Blades slipped back the catches and lifted up the lid. More body parts wrapped in bloody brown paper. Why had the murderer bothered to cover them like this? Possibly he had wanted to stop blood seeping out, which would have been awkward when he was carrying the case about. It did give Blades the revolting chore of separating paper from body part. Then he found it, what he had not expected to find though it had been what he had hoped for. This was it. The other hand. And on it. There. Yes. Just there. An unbelievable piece of carelessness from their careful murderer: shining clearly, even in this half-light, a silver ring. Perhaps the murderer had been far more upset by chopping up a body than he had expected. He must have been, to miss that. And this could tell them if this was Emma or not. Despite the blood and gore, despite the

mud and the sting from where brambles had pulled at his
skin, there was a smile on Blades' face.

CHAPTER THIRTY-NINE

Blades was seated in front of Moffat's desk again but this time he was repressing a grin. He wasn't even struggling with the hard seat or the upright back but was seated in a relaxed position, leaning back, with his legs crossed and hands relaxed in his lap. Moffat was not at ease.

'Russell Parkes?' Moffat said. 'I told you to stay away from him.'

'I did, but proof turned up elsewhere. We found the body and we've found links to him. Why are we supposed to ignore that?'

Moffat gave Blades a sour stare but looked at a loss for words. Then he spoke as if the statement was being dragged from him physically and causing great pain. 'Obviously, no one gets away with murder. But you have to be absolutely sure of your proof after the conversation that we had.'

'Pressure was being put on you, sir, but, as you've just said, no one is above the law.'

'And no one is above competent supervision.' Moffat spoke quietly but with meaning.

'As you say, sir.'

Blades waited for a lead from Moffat that would allow him to present his case, but Moffat looked as if he did not want to listen to anything. Moffat's thumb was twisting itself into a hole in the desk in front of him, and Blades wondered if Moffat realised this.

'Go on,' Moffat said. 'The conclusive proof.'

'We were searching for the missing body parts.'

'A search you were told to close down.'

'We had, sir, but we had a tip off. They turned up a hundred yards away from where we'd finished searching in a copse by the railway bridge.'

'And?'

'There were two suitcases hidden there, with parts of a body wrapped in brown paper. One of the cases was half open, which was why some animal was able to drag out the first hand that we found. It only dragged it a few hundred yards away, as I say. If that.'

'So, why hadn't you found it before?'

Blades ignored that remark. 'We've found it now,' he replied. 'The other hand had a ring on the index finger, a silver ring with a love-heart motif, which Emma's parents have identified as belonging to Emma.'

For the first time, Moffat looked half-pleased.

'So, we have proof of who the murder victim is. And the cause of death?'

'The murderer hasn't allowed us to establish that. Not all of the body's there. Time of death does fit in with the day that Emma disappeared – as far as it can be established. In other words, there's no reason to suppose it doesn't.'

'Can they even be as definite as that? The body's dismembered.'

'They say so.'

'And the argument for it being murder?'

'The fact the body was chopped up and disposed of suggests it.'

'Everything else being equal, but all right, you can establish corpus delicti. But what makes you think the murderer was Russell Parkes?'

'One of the suitcases is identical with one that we know he bought. We have a witness to that from a local store. Russell Parkes' alibi for the time of Emma's disappearance was a lie, and Russell initially lied about having any relationship with Emma, though we now know he had one.'

'You have means? Opportunity? Motive?'

'Means have not been established as we do not know exactly how Emma died, but he is physically capable of murdering Emma. There was a big difference between them in terms of height and strength.'

'Opportunity?'

'He saw her regularly. She would certainly allow him entrance if he called, and he has no alibi.'

'Motive?'

'Perhaps if we ask him, he'll tell us. He was in debt. She was about to come into money. There may have been arguments around that.'

'Do you think your case is conclusive?'

'The fact the suitcase was his clinches it.'

Moffat drummed his fingers. 'This will make us unpopular in certain quarters,' he said.

'And even more unpopular in the press if we don't act on it, sir.'

There was an indecisiveness on Moffat's face that Blades had not seen before.

'We have a witness who saw a man carrying those suitcases out of the Roots' house,' Blades insisted.

'Wasn't that the man with "funny eyes"?' Moffat said. 'Has Russell Parkes got those?'

'You were right, sir, when you said he saw the man from too far away to make reliable comments about his eyes. Otherwise, his description does fit Russell Parkes. Perhaps if we did an identity parade with Russell Parkes in it instead of Duggan, he would be picked out. We haven't done one of those.'

Moffat walked over to the window and looked out. It was a dull, uninteresting view of the street outside, and Blades wondered how that could be helpful at all, though probably Moffat wasn't taking it in. Blades noticed that when Moffat next turned to Blades, his face had found its decisiveness.

'Right,' he said. 'Get that parade done. And question him.'

CHAPTER FORTY

Blades and Peacock stood in Birtleby Police Station, awaiting another identity parade. Blades was happier about this one. The six 'suspects' were all of similar height, build, and age, and eyes were not a factor. The man seen with the suitcases from a distance had not been described as having a gold tooth, but Blades supposed Russell Parkes' mouth might not have been open. The men stood looking bored if mildly apprehensive, except Parkes, who had adopted a careless attitude that to Blades made him look guilty. The apprentice butcher, Alan Atkinson, was led in and stared around him like a rabbit caught in headlights. Blades supposed this was a big occasion for him and wondered what his father had said prior to his turning up that day. Blades walked over to him and spoke. 'Just relax,' he said, 'and be sure of what you're doing. If you're not sure, don't make a positive identification. If you are, put your hand on the right shoulder of the man you're identifying. Remember. It's not you who's on trial here. It's them.'

The boy nodded, though his face remained pale and drawn. He began his walk up the line. He walked slowly, peering at each in turn, and his expression did not change once, all the way up the line, from one of fierce concentration. The expressions on the faces of the 'suspects' varied, from the apprehensive to the impatient. All avoided looking directly at the butcher's boy. Then the boy stopped, turned, and walked back down the line. When he reached Russell Parkes, he stopped, and placed his right hand on his shoulder, briefly, then stepped back hurriedly as if afraid of what Parkes might do to him for singling him out. Then the boy turned and looked at Blades as if for instruction.

'Thank you,' Blades said, and signalled to a constable who led the boy out of the room.

Blades turned to Peacock. 'That went well,' he said, to which Peacock nodded.

The line remained in place while the next witness was brought in. Reg Bright was a particularly short man, only about five foot one, Blades estimated, and he had to look up at a row of tall men; Blades wondered how intimidating that would be for him. But he need not have worried. Reg held himself with his usual air of cockiness. Indeed, he looked impatient to get started. Blades nodded and Reg started on a trot down the line, peering imperiously at each as he walked past them. They looked nervous as Reg paced past them, but they all managed to avoid returning his stare. Reg reached the end of the line and raked another look down it, which was almost like a broadside in its aggressiveness. Then he strode back down the line and put his hand firmly on the shoulder of one of the 'suspects'. The man winced and looked shocked but there was no change in Reg's attitude of smugness. He turned and shot a look at Blades as if to say, 'That's me finished. Can I go home now?' Blades gave a nod and the constable led Reg out.

Blades looked at the man Reg had indicated. Blades knew him. He was a constable from Fossmouth who'd been drafted in for this, and the expression on his face suggested he was duly offended at being mistaken for a murderer. Blades thanked the men in the identity parade and dismissed them all except Russell Parkes, who was led by another police constable to the interview room.

Blades turned to Peacock. 'A pity only one of them picked him out.'

'You didn't think one was enough the last time,' Peacock said.

'With all the rest we've got on Parkes, the proof stacks up well enough with one identification.'

'So, we charge Russell Parkes?'

'It won't please Moffat considering what he's told us in the past, but we'd be derelict in our duty if we didn't.'

But, after Blades returned to his desk, he found a new report sitting there for him to look at, and, when he had read it, he did wonder if it would turn his neatly solved case entirely on its head, which would be a pity. He had been wanting to put one over on Moffat.

CHAPTER FORTY-ONE

The summons to the police station filled Thomas with dread. He had always tried to keep his nose clean. How had things ended up like this? Amelia's snide remarks did not help. According to her, it was all his fault. And why was that? So, he had flirted with Louisa. How did that justify the police hauling him in?

'You're at your difficult age,' Amelia shrieked at him. 'I should have kept a better eye on you.'

Avoiding Amelia's tongue mattered to Thomas, though respectability meant as much. Birtleby was a small town and it held his livelihood. He would never actually misbehave here. Flirting with Louisa was harmless enough. In any case, she had started it. He would not allow it to lead to anything, so why resist the temptation? Amelia had lost interest in sex, something he did not understand but had to accept. How did she think that might affect a healthy man? He did have feelings building inside him at times, powerful, overwhelming ones. Flirting was a harmless outlet for them. Amelia occasionally did allow his advances, though she made it seem a favour, and left him feeling he had behaved towards her like an animal. But it was always such a long wait till the next time. Did Amelia not understand how difficult that was?

He did take advantage of opportunities with other women when he was away on business trips. There had been that young woman in Leeds called Alice. She was particularly fetching, not unlike Emma with that slight, gamine-like appearance, and those brunette waves that curved down over her forehead. Her skin was almost translucent; it seemed to shimmer when he touched it, and yes, she had let him touch it. That had made him feel young and alive, which was a sensation he seemed to need. And it had led to sex, which had been thrilling and invigorating, but that feeling of virility that surged through him had to be put in a box when he came back. He did not have affairs in Birtleby. That was why it had hurt so much when Emma had started that argument before his trip away with Amelia. She had told him then in no uncertain terms to keep away from Louisa. If Emma had any idea how hard he worked at keeping his lust under control, she would not speak to him like that – or she might talk even more sternly, he supposed. In any case, her anger with him had been severe. It was not as if he took liberties with Emma herself. She did not allow that, so anger had surged inside him as she lectured. The temptation to pull his arm back and strike her was almost overwhelming. But he had stopped himself. And here he was, approaching a police station with Amelia, ready to be questioned about the murder of Emma Simpson. Someone had done it, but it had not been him. He could see why they might suspect him. He had always thought it must be dreadful for a person to be tried for something he had not done, and he was in terror of that happening to him now. Amelia gave him an accusing glance as he opened the door to the police station, but he did not return it, just walked into whatever hell lay in front of him.

When he walked over to Sergeant Peacock at the front desk, Peacock acknowledged him with a nod, wrote his and Amelia's names down, and gestured to some seats lined against the wall. Thomas had trudged over with Amelia and sat down with an undisguised sigh as he looked around him at the painted grey wooden walls of the police station with its solitary decoration of a round clock in mahogany with a white face and black Roman numerals. Thomas noticed the time. He took his pocket watch out to check and noticed that they had arrived early by five minutes. No problem there. Thomas thought back to the blustering, self-righteous person he had been in his first meeting with Blades as he had thundered into the man for breaking down their front door. He had been unnerved since then. He heard Amelia sigh beside him. He hoped she would not burst into tears again. Then he started thinking of his own behaviour. He must not lose his temper when faced with Blades' questions. He had met those before, when he had been duly rattled by the accuracy of Blades' knowledge of the row with Emma and the flirtations with Louisa.

Sergeant Peacock was still busy at the desk with files, though there was something aimless in the way he was shifting them about that suggested pretence. Thomas supposed Peacock could be there to watch them. He did glance over now and again as they sat on the uncomfortable wooden chairs, shifting every so often and staring into space.

The door to the station was then opened and a draught from outside, and a self-important sergeant, came in. With a cursory nod between him and Sergeant Peacock, he marched past the desk and towards an inner office. There was a murmur of voices, one of which Thomas recognized as Blades', then the door was closed, and Thomas presumed the conversation was continued behind it. After a few minutes, the policeman returned, and gave another nod to Peacock before disappearing elsewhere in the building. He had purposefully ignored Thomas and Amelia, but it had not been without an element of scorn somehow, and Thomas had felt something ominous about him that he could not define.

He looked at Amelia again. He was feeling worn down and resentful, but he was in a situation together with her, whosever fault it was, and he was not without sympathy for her. She was innocent enough, if usually a bit boring, and, he sometimes thought, inadequate. He wished he had not looked for diversion elsewhere but been a better husband to her. He thought back to the fractiousness of the drive over and was glad the flow of words she had unleashed then had dried up. There had been nothing weak about her then. He had not known before how assertive she could be. He had always known that mouse-like exterior did not give a true impression – despite his blustering bossiness, she had never stopped giving adept and timely nags in return – but the venom she had just unleashed on him was new. He was glad he had taken such care to keep his affairs elsewhere so secret. She was angry enough about what she knew about his behaviour. What would she be like if she knew about what he had been up to? Then, the thought occurred. She didn't know, did she? He glanced across at her then away. He hated this, sitting here with nothing to do but fret – and fret again.

He looked across at Peacock. He decided Peacock really did have nothing to do behind that desk but listen to them – if they were unguarded enough to speak.

Then the door opened, and another policeman walked in, another sergeant. He also nodded to Peacock before marching through towards Blades' office. There was what sounded like another long confab in there before he emerged, then disappeared elsewhere in the station, not without successfully glancing disdain at the assembled suspects on his way past. Thomas supposed this to-ing and fro-ing might be normal. Blades must have supervisory duties over uniform. All the same, these passing policemen chilled him.

Then the door opened again, as Alfred Duggan strolled in and presented himself to Peacock. There was nothing anxious about him, Thomas thought. He looked as if he thought he was doing Peacock a favour by gracing him with his presence.

'I'm here to see Inspector Blades,' he announced.

Drat, Thomas thought. Would they have to wait till Duggan had talked with him?

'I'll let him know you're here, sir,' Peacock replied. 'Please, take a seat.'

But Thomas noticed that Peacock did not leave his desk to announce anything to anybody, just returned to the same file. Duggan sat right beside Thomas. The boldness of the man. 'I see you're here,' Duggan said. 'You're the ones who did it, are you?'

'You mind your tongue,' Thomas said. 'Speak respectfully when you're talking to people who are respectable, if the likes of you knows what that means.'

'I do know,' Duggan said. 'It means you talk self-righteously after church on a Sunday and do what you like for the rest of the week.'

Thomas smarted at the comment, as, he noticed, did Amelia.

'For a convicted bigamist you speak in a self-righteous way yourself,' he replied.

'My sin's on my face,' Duggan replied, 'an honest appreciation of the fair sex, if that's a sin.'

Thomas noticed Peacock was grinning with amusement. Amelia was looking offended by the mere proximity of Duggan.

Thomas felt his frustrations rising inside him. 'Did you kill her?' he asked Duggan. The question surprised Thomas himself. He had not expected to be so forthright.

'I wouldn't need to be violent with Emma to get what I wanted out of her,' Duggan replied.

Thomas felt rage surge inside him, as he considered what Duggan intended him to understand by that, but the most sensible thing to do was control his anger, especially as Duggan was only amusing himself. That tone was light, and teasing, though all the more annoying for that. The thought of aiming a punch at Duggan appealed but not the consequences. Thomas was continuing to seethe in his seat when the door opened again, and another young man walked in. Thomas did not know him but thought he looked not unlike Duggan, being about the same height and build, though Thomas noticed that when he flashed his unconvincing smile at Sergeant Peacock, there was the gleam of a gold tooth in the top right of his mouth that was entirely his own.

'Russell Parkes. I've an appointment with Inspector Blades at ten,' he said in a tone which, like Duggan's, was intended to be confident, but which, in his case, sounded false.

Did he say ten? Thomas thought. Did they all have an appointment with Blades for the same time? What was going on here? But Peacock did not correct the man, just nodded at him, and gestured to the row of chairs the rest of them were seated in. Parkes walked over, glanced towards Duggan, and seated himself on the other side of Amelia and well away from Duggan.

'You could at least acknowledge me,' Duggan said.

'Oh, hello, Alfred. Didn't see you seated there. Are you being questioned about bigamy again?'

Another one on edge, Thomas thought. Hardly surprising with a murder to be investigated.

'I didn't do it, you know,' Duggan said.

'Do what?' Parkes replied. 'The description of "it" could cover a lot in your case.'

'Shop you to the Leighton Insurance Company.'

'Don't know what you're talking about.'

'You lost that job yourself. It had nothing to do with me.'

'What is it you're trying to suggest? I didn't lose it. I left for another job.'

'So you say.'

'I do.'

Thomas noticed even more the similarity between Duggan and Parkes – in their accents and mannerisms, and rudeness – as well as their appearance. Then he realised that, of course, as this must be another young man that Emma had known, this must be her type. A pity. She had been worth more than them.

'Is that Thomas Root?' Parkes said to Duggan as he pointed at Thomas.

'That's him,' Duggan replied.

'Randy old sod, aren't you?' Parkes said to Thomas.

'I beg your pardon?' Thomas replied.

'Emma told me all about you. Couldn't keep your hands to yourself when young female staff were around, could you?'

Thomas opened his mouth to reply, but, before he could, Duggan spoke. 'Is that what Emma told you? She said just the same to me.'

'I didn't misbehave with Emma,' Thomas said.

'Really?' Duggan replied.

'It's a bit rum this, isn't it?' Russell said, suddenly totally off topic.

'What is?' Duggan asked. Both Thomas and Amelia looked at him, mystified.

'Here we are, three sets of suspects all gathered in the same place to be questioned, and with nothing to do but annoy each other.'

Both Duggan and Amelia nodded. Thomas was bristling. Everything was getting under his skin. 'What do you think the idea is?' he asked.

'To try to find the murderer?' Duggan replied.

'Having us all seated here together like this?' Russell said. 'I expect we're supposed to get on each other's nerves. Which we are doing. And then, I should think, they're hoping we'll give ourselves away. Perhaps the murderer should just confess and give all the rest of us a break.' He turned to Thomas. 'Was it you?'

'How dare you, the likes of you?' Thomas said.

Duggan considered this, then said, 'I wouldn't put it past you, Russell. You were after money from Emma. She did tell me. Is that why you killed her? Because she said no?'

'I didn't, did I?' Russell said. 'In any case, I'd have had to beat you to it. It's not that much of a step from humiliating women for your pleasure to killing them.'

'You might know that,' Duggan said. 'I don't.'

'Stop bickering.' The voice cut through the air like a knife. The men stopped arguing and looked at Amelia.

After a pause, Duggan said, 'One of us knows the answer. Perhaps they ought to own up now.'

'We ought to be more careful about what we say,' Thomas said. 'That sergeant is writing it all down.' He had noticed the black notebook that Peacock held within the file and that he was scribbling furiously in.

They all stared at Peacock, who stared back, and grinned.

'Or did none of us do it?' Duggan asked of no one in particular.

'I didn't,' Thomas said.

'Why does Blades think you might have done?'

'Amelia and I were the last people to see her alive – that he knows of. And we did have a row with her. Emma had been shopping me to Amelia – about Louisa, though. Not her.'

'And that's how we got into this,' Amelia said. 'He can't keep his hands to himself.'

'And did you kill her?' Duggan asked.

'Of course, I didn't,' Thomas replied.

'There's no of course about any of it,' Duggan said. 'You'll have to convince Blades you're innocent. Have you got your answers ready?'

'Obviously not,' Thomas said. 'I don't need to lie and make up stories. I didn't do it.'

'What makes Blades think you might have done it, Alfred?' Russell asked.

'A lack of imagination,' Duggan said. 'He can't find the real killer.'

'But why you?' Russell said.

'I knew her, I suppose. And someone killed her.'

'He's asked me about the Saturday. What's so significant about that?' Russell asked.

'That's the last time Emma was seen alive,' Thomas said. 'Amelia and I drove off to Ramshead for a week's holiday – I remembered it was about ten, but it was probably nearer eleven. So, when did you see her?' Thomas asked Duggan.

'Ah,' Duggan said. 'I don't suppose I should answer that, not that it matters considering you did it,' he said to Russell. 'You hate me enough. You'd bump off Emma just because she was my girl.'

'You thought she was your girl, you mean. Why was she seeing me?'

'And why do the police think you did it?' Thomas asked Russell.

'I've no alibi for the Saturday.'

'So, any one of us could have done it?' Thomas said.

'Three different suspects,' Russell said.

'Unless it's four,' Duggan said, looking at Amelia.

'I was wondering when you were going to get around to me,' Amelia said. 'Inspector Blades does think I might have been angry with Emma because she was leading Thomas on.'

'Except Emma wasn't,' Thomas said.

'But one of us did murder her,' Duggan said.

'According to the police,' Russell said.

'And what are we going to do about that?' Duggan said.

At that moment, the interior door opened, and the room went quiet as Blades came in and looked at them. 'Bring Russell Parkes in,' he said.

Silence fell after Russell Parkes had been taken away. Thomas noticed that Sergeant Ryan had replaced Peacock behind the desk, and he presumed Ryan would now be writing relevant notes of any conversation they had.

The clock ticked. A car rumbled past the window. Sergeant Ryan coughed. Duggan shifted in his seat. Amelia frowned at Thomas as he moved his hand to take out a Woodbine, before changing his mind.

'Do you think he's getting anything out of Russell?' Thomas said.

Two pairs of eyes bored through him. Thomas decided to keep quiet. No one said anything for a while. Duggan rose from his seat and paced to the window and back. Then he turned towards Thomas and spoke.

'He should have been questioning Russell a lot earlier.'

'I didn't know about Russell,' Thomas said. 'He's a surprise.'

'I thought there was someone,' Amelia said. 'I knew she practised her music. At first, I thought it was with a group. Then I thought it must be with another young woman.'

'You didn't ask her?' Thomas said.

'I didn't place that much importance on it,' Amelia said.

'I don't suppose she wanted me to find out,' Duggan said.

They all fell silent again. After an eternity, the door opened, and Russell was shown back through. Thomas studied him but could tell nothing from his demeanour about what might have happened when he was in Blades' sanctum. The suspects waited in fretful silence. Then two more policemen entered from outside, both sergeants. Thomas had not realised there were so many of them in Birtleby. Perhaps it was a procession that had been arranged for the purpose of intimidating the suspects even more.

Blades called out for the Roots to enter.

CHAPTER FORTY-TWO

As he and Peacock left the office and entered the corridor, Blades was struck by the intent look on the faces that swivelled towards him. Thomas in particular looked terrified. He had given Thomas and Amelia a thorough interrogation when he called them through. Though he had covered no new ground, it had obviously had an effect. And Blades was ready to go further now all the evidence had arrived.

At that moment, the door to the station opened and Musgrave walked in.

On cue, Blades thought, Musgrave, with his usual imperious glance and swaggering stride.

'Hello, John,' Blades said to him. 'Good of you to come.'

'Good of you to send for me.'

'Have a seat.'

Musgrave glanced along the row of suspects. His eyebrows arched in surprise.

'I take it you'll have news to spill when you've time?' he said.

'Possibly by the end of the morning,' Blades replied.

'Meanwhile?'

Blades gave him a cryptic smile.

'It's good to see you, John. Take a seat.'

Musgrave gave this a moment's thought, then said, 'As you wish,' then sat down.

Blades noticed his suspects glancing between him and Musgrave, then back again.

Then Blades said, 'Let's face it. I haven't always felt in charge of this investigation. It's time I took control.'

Blades noticed the indignation on Amelia's face; he supposed she was still smarting from the interrogation.

'You can't blame us for your problems,' she said. 'You've had nothing but my co-operation.'

'You haven't tried to mislead me?' Blades said. 'What was that story about port being spilled? We found no trace of that, only the blood you said could not possibly have been there.'

'I—' Amelia spluttered. Perplexity had quickly replaced the self-righteousness. 'But I didn't see how you could have found any blood in the parlour.'

'So, don't make something up,' Blades said.

He noticed that Amelia, sensibly, did not reply. He continued. 'We know Emma died just after she faced you with your husband's misbehaviour and insisted you do something about it.'

'But I didn't—' Amelia replied.

'And it is when Emma was killed,' Blades said. 'Which makes you suspect number one.'

'I've told you my husband would not behave like that.'

'I said you, not your husband. Did you lash out in a temper?'

'I'm not the one with a temper,' Amelia said.

'You mean Thomas is?' Blades said.

Thomas's face showed clearly what he thought of the sound of that. Amelia was reduced to staring back at Blades.

'Which still doesn't mean it couldn't have been you.'

Thomas was staring at him in impotent fury but Blades was glad to see him still seated and still silent.

'And for long enough I thought it must be you,' Blades said to Amelia. 'You're the picture of the downtrodden wife, who puts up with things over and over – and then yet again – until, finally, it is too much and she snaps.'

'You thought it might be me?' Amelia asked. 'You don't now?'

There was relief on her face.

Blades did not reply to that, but simply spread his gaze around the suspects arrayed before him.

'I've had to give thought to so many suspects,' Blades said. 'They've been strewn all over the place with gleeful abandon. In fact, it puzzled me that there could be so many. It's not the usual thing with murder cases. It's a bit obvious who did most murders because there was only one person who, in the first place, knew the victim well enough to be motivated to murder them, and, two, could possibly have done it.'

He threw an accusing look at them all, before settling his eyes on Thomas.

'And obviously I had to question Amelia particularly carefully, as she could have said more to give you away.'

'Me?' Thomas glared at Blades. 'But you've asked me the same questions over and over, and I've answered every one of them. Truthfully,' he emphasised, 'because I didn't do it.'

'But you fit the crime as well,' Blades replied. 'A man of a difficult age faced with the temptation of an attractive young woman around him all the time.'

'Rubbish,' Thomas said.

'Was Emma talking to you about the fact you were misbehaving with Louisa? Or did you try to force yourself on Emma? A young woman like her up to no good with a man like Alfred Duggan. Did you think she was asking for it really? Did you think she deserved it?'

'No. She didn't. And I didn't. I've told you before, I liked Emma. I wouldn't do anything like that to her.'

'But the question's still there,' Blades replied. 'The overbearing arrogant employer so used to getting his own way. Why not take that one small step further and get your own way about something personal you really wanted?'

'You've no proof of that.'

'Which I need to have. But, on the other hand, you haven't proved you didn't do that.'

'I don't have to.'

'No. But I need to find some way of dismissing you from my inquiries when you're sitting up begging to be considered a suspect in the way you are. It doesn't take six hours to travel from Birtleby to Ramshead, and you still haven't given a convincing explanation for how you spent all that time that day. And you lied to us. You said Emma had just been behaving as usual, that she did not seem any different from her normal self when you left, but that was the same day that you had the row with her. In my experience it's guilty people who lie, Mr Root.'

'Not just. No, not just,' Thomas said. 'All right, I lied,' he admitted. 'But I didn't kill her. Really, I didn't.'

Blades looked at Thomas's face and, for the first time, showed some pity.

'So you say, but you could have helped yourself and us much better by being open with us from the beginning.'

Thomas was nodding as he looked back at him.

'But your lies pale in significance against those of Russell Parkes.'

Russell sat up in his chair and looked askance at Blades.

'Now look here,' he said.

'I heard an almost endless list of those from you,' Blades said. 'You said you hardly knew Emma, yet you were often in her company as she and you met to practise music together, if that's what you were doing.'

'Of course it was,' Parkes said. 'Emma had fine musical abilities.'

'You gave a false alibi. You said you were with Rose Weller all day on the Saturday when, in fact, you met up with her on the Friday.'

'An easy enough mistake to make. We were confused about the day.'

'You have no alibi for the day of Emma's disappearance.' Blades was looking directly at Russell Parkes who now could only stare at the floor.

'Have you?'

'No,' Parkes muttered.

'You have gambling debts, and what makes that suspicious is the fact you have a conviction for assault on a young woman over money.'

'I've explained that,' Parkes said. 'I've explained all of it. Why do you have to keep on bringing up the same things over and over?'

'You're the type to have done it,' Blades said. 'You're a womaniser who makes use of women simply for his own ends – which could be taken one step further and lead to murder.'

'Which it didn't,' Parkes said. 'So, you can't have any proof I killed her.'

'If only any of you knew how to behave when being investigated by the police, it would help. If you're suspicious, and all of you are, we have to learn enough to dismiss you from our investigations or convict you. And every one of you has lied over and over again, making yourselves look even more guilty. It's not like when your husband or wife – or father or mother, employer or teacher – questions you about something they think you've done. It's not enough to make up any excuse that comes into your head. This has been a serious legal investigation, and your deceptions have wasted my time.'

'But we can all go now?' Parkes said.

'No,' Blades replied.

'Do I get my story now?' Musgrave asked.

'Unless you are the story,' Blades replied.

'What?' Musgrave said, and the cheroot dropped out of his mouth.

'Because there might be a case against you.'

'Me?'

'You've been so helpful. But I've often wondered why. Instead of always being able to follow up on where I've been wanting to go with this investigation, I've kept coming across you trying to lead me in a different direction. And the question is why.'

'Hang on. I've been of assistance. I've given information in order to help you. Who told you where to find the body?'

'And who told you? How did you know where it was?'

'I've said. I can't reveal sources.'

'A useful excuse. You're the one who kept pointing me towards Russell Parkes. You knew about his connection with Emma. You told me about his problems with the Leighton Insurance Company. You knew about his alibi being false.'

'That must have been useful. Are you complaining about that?'

'But how did you know?'

'I can't–'

'–reveal sources. Perhaps it was Emma herself who had told you all about Parkes.'

'Emma?'

'Because you knew Emma as well, didn't you? You're not the only one who has informants and we've done interviews all over Birtleby. You're distinctive. How many people go about with that hat and chewing that cheroot all day?'

'I–'

'You could just admit it. We can prove it.'

'I-I suppose. I didn't know her well, though.' Musgrave was deflated. His fleshy face sagged. 'I did meet her a few times, that was all. I knew her through one of the girls in the office. That's not an offence.'

'But it does mean you're someone who needs to be actively dismissed from the inquiry. How did you know where Emma's body was?'

'I–well–' But an answer obviously did not immediately spring from Musgrave's tongue.

'I've looked at everyone else. Let's look at you. What goes with that overblown cynical journalist act? A personality that looks for and craves attention. What better way to gain warped pleasure than from murdering someone and framing someone else for the murder, then pointing the police in his direction?'

'That's slander.'

'It's a question. I'm running a murder inquiry. Where were you getting all of your information from?'

Musgrave's mouth was wide open now. He reached for another cheroot, thought better of it, then put it back in his pocket. 'I suppose I'd better say something before you finish your case against me.' But Musgrave paused for thought again. Then he said, 'Yes. I'd better tell you. I found out from Duggan.'

Blades gave Duggan a fierce look. 'So, not only was Duggan turning up in person to send my investigation on wild goose trails, he was sending you to do the same. And he knew exactly where the body was to be found.'

Blades was examining Duggan, as everyone else was doing. Duggan had turned his luminous blue eyes on Blades. That wholehearted smile was on his face, and his picture of innocence looked like a challenge.

'You could have done it, Mr Duggan. A lot of facts point to it, and your psychology does. That's a wandering, disorganized mind you have.'

Duggan's eyes widened at this. The vacant, irritating smile disappeared to be replaced by a frown.

'It fascinates me. Women are strongly attracted to you, and it draws you to them as much as the other way around. You can't say no to them – even if you tried, which I suspect you don't.'

Duggan's smile returned at that. 'You sound jealous, Inspector Blades. Are you struggling to find anyone to philander with?'

Blades returned the smile but he knew his was icy. 'And there's no way any sensible person would have expected to get away with bigamy in the way you did. Your second marriage was to someone who stayed only a few miles away. How could you have expected to get away with that?'

'Women usually believe what I tell them.' Then Duggan laughed, yawned, and reached in his waistcoat pocket for a cigarette.

Blades was the one who frowned now. 'You were lucky your first wife didn't divorce you. You deserved it. I was surprised by that. She only decided on a divorce relatively recently, when she became convinced you'd gone that huge step further and committed murder. Because it looks that way. A bizarre, extremely emotional person with poor restraint, with strong links to a murdered woman.'

'She didn't mean it though. She wouldn't have gone through with a divorce.'

But Blades noticed he did not deny the murder.

'Are you really so sure of your power over women, Alfred Duggan?' he asked.

Duggan lit his cigarette, drew in a lungful of smoke which he made a point of luxuriating in before replying. 'Of course. Isn't everybody?'

'It was you I first suspected. You insisted on having so much attention from me. You kept turning up at the station. You changed your statement, which was bizarre. That made both statements unbelievable and unlikely to help you. Then you kept on coming up with information. And information that didn't make sense. You pointed me at Russell Parkes by suggesting a motive that would never hold water. He murdered her for money she didn't have. Then I began to understand why your first wife didn't leave you. It was because you usually don't make sense, do you?'

Which was so obvious now as he looked at Alfred Duggan. That relaxed and arrogant pose was entirely unsuited to his situation.

'She felt she ought to stay with you to look out for her husband. I found out why when I looked up your medical records. Oh, yes, they arrived eventually. You suffered from a serious head wound in the war.'

Blades noticed the sharp intake of breath from the other suspects but his gaze was on Duggan as he studied the unconcerned eyes and the empty smile.

'Oh yes,' Blades said. 'It completely changed your character, as happened, you might be interested to hear, to a man called Phineas Gage, a foreman working on a railway line in the USA in the nineteenth century.'

Alfred's look was mystified. 'Just what has anyone called Phineas Gage got to do with me?'

'He had an accident,' Blades continued. 'Before that, his firm thought of him as their most reliable employee; and he was extremely popular with the men he worked with. Then the unfortunate man had a bolt go clean through his skull when he was working. He didn't manage to hold down his job after that.'

Alfred now shot Blades a look of mockery.

'He was unpredictable, followed whims as they occurred to him, without thinking any of them through, and he didn't even notice the effect any plans of his had on other people. And you suffered from a war wound, didn't you, Alfred?'

'A lot of people were wounded in that war. What of it?'

'A bullet went completely through your brain. You should be dead. Nobody understood why you survived but you did.'

'Is that a crime?'

'Before that, you were a steady husband and a reliable soldier, a sergeant that your officers thought well of and could rely on. After that, your behaviour became completely flaky and unpredictable, particularly that temper of yours. And they said you were completely unable to tell truth from falsehood. You were given a dishonourable discharge from the army, after which you had the greatest difficulty in settling into civilian life. It wasn't Russell Parkes who was in trouble about discrepancies in his accounts. It was you. Yes. I did find that out. Your brother-in-law got you your present job. Otherwise you wouldn't have one. And you became a bigamist. And you killed Emma.'

Alfred said nothing in reply, just breathed in more smoke and breathed it out slowly.

'As to why you killed Emma, only you know the answer to that, but you do like having power over women. I should think the problem with Emma was she was too independent, and that she said no, and did it in such a way as to challenge that arrogance of yours in a way you did not like at all.'

Alfred was not yet cowed. There was even a sneer on his face. 'You'll never prove it.'

'People keep telling me that. But I'm a policeman. I look for proof and here it is, Alfred. Have you seen this before?' Then Blades took a bracelet from his pocket.

Now Alfred's poise was shaken. He stared at the silver chain bracelet with horror. 'How did you get that?' he said.

'You do recognize it, then? Yes, you would. This is Emma's bracelet. It even has her initials on it. And the initials of her husband. It must have been one of her most precious memories of him. All that work you put into trying to divert attention from yourself. You even had poor Musgrave primed to do that for you. And all the time I wasted on Russell Parkes. You've been a diligent rogue at least, but you're under arrest now, Alfred. I'm charging you with the murder of Emma Simpson. You do not have to say anything but whatever you do say will be taken down and may be used as evidence against you.'

'But I–' Alfred started to say. 'How did you get hold of it?'

'We have a warrant to search your premises, Alfred. We had a warrant to search everyone's place. I had my theory, of course, but I wanted to be sure, which is why we invited everyone else here, to get everyone's place done at the same time. We knew we wouldn't have to invite you, Alfred, not after you'd heard about our little meeting, which I made sure of. You'd just be along. I was almost taken in by the theory it was the man you put so much effort into directing me to, Russell Parkes. But we didn't find Emma's bracelet in his place. We found it in yours.'

The look of helplessness that now lay on Duggan's face was the most satisfying thing Blades had seen in a long time. Then Duggan looked around him for a moment as if he was considering making a bolt for it, but there were more than enough policemen in Birtleby Police Station to subdue Alfred Duggan.

CHAPTER FORTY-THREE

It was the end of the case and the end of the day. Blades was standing looking at the noticeboard in the meeting room. Behind him the policemen under his command waited for his attention. Mostly, of course, they waited for the chance to finish and go home. Blades' thoughts were, for the moment, on Emma again. He had gazed at the picture of Emma smiling from beyond the grave all through this inquiry. On his wall was the most recent photograph there had been of her and it had been taken a year before her death. It showed a young woman in her prime, smiling confidently at life, with all the expectation of youth. She had tugged at his heart strings as she smiled at him through every stage of the investigation.

Beside her, on the noticeboard, there were also photographs of suitcases in situ, of the bathroom where the body had been cut up, and the parlour where the blow had been struck. There were also photographs of all the different suspects with comments marked beside them, and links drawn between them. All the things that had baffled and bemused them had been clearly displayed so that there was no mistaking what their investigation had to work its way through, and he was glad to have reached the end of it. When he turned to face his colleagues, it was with a smile on his face for the first time in a while.

The whole team was gathered there, all the sergeants and constables who'd been involved, well, most of them. Those who'd been seconded from elsewhere for the search for the body had returned to their own stations some time ago. Beer had been poured and uniformed men sat with glasses in hands and smug grins on faces. It was time to celebrate. They had earned the right to do that. Blades raised his own tankard. They were not, of course, supposed to drink beer in the station but Blades thought it did no harm to be human on occasions like this.

'Congratulations, team,' he said. 'We got him!'

And a triumphant cheer was heard from all. Then some started sipping beer. All were grinning.

'Glory be,' Blades said as he sipped from his own. 'And a well-earned thanks.'

There were a lot of happy faces in that room and the happiest, Blades was sure, was his own.

'A great speech you gave our suspects at the end,' Peacock said.

'A well-led investigation,' Ryan added.

'Thank you,' Blades said. 'But I couldn't have done anything without all of you.'

More grins were shared amongst them.

'I was sure it was Parkes,' Peacock said.

'I wish it had been,' Blades said. 'That would have sorted out his powerful friends.'

Peacock laughed. 'And made Moffat look bad.'

'Which we wouldn't want to do, of course.'

There was a general chuckle at that.

'So, it wasn't Parkes' suitcase the body was in?' Peacock said.

'Oh no,' Blades said. 'Though we could have continued thinking that if we hadn't turned up his own in his home. There's one thing for sure. His case couldn't be in two places at the same time – under his bed and in our evidence room. No. That was a tale.'

'Where did the tip-off come from?' Peacock asked.

'Didn't I say? An anonymous phone call, Duggan I expect, saying one of the cases was identical to one Parkes had bought in Houghton's in town. And the description matched. And the time he bought it fitted in. Oh, I thought we had Parkes for the murder at that point.'

'What made you change your mind?' Ryan asked.

'The report on Alfred Duggan, the one that told me about his head wound and the change in his character. All that muddled thinking coming from him, it fitted everything that had been going on. A person like that was awry enough to try to put the blame on someone else in exactly the way that Duggan was doing it. Though you've always got to prove suspects guilty. Which is why I was so pleased when we turned up the bracelet at his place.'

'You didn't send for Duggan, though?' Ryan asked.

'That was taking a chance,' Peacock said. 'He might not have turned up.'

'Didn't I tell you? He was being watched. If he hadn't come in, I'd have sent for him. But I knew he'd be there. I had him worked out.'

'Very satisfying, sir.'

'Definitely.'

Blades sank some more beer. He turned his head to look at the noticeboard again. Emma was still there, smiling, but that grin seemed to be sharing their triumph now, and he told himself there was thanks in her eyes – though he knew there wasn't really. He just wished there was. Photographs didn't come to life like that.

'Here's to the end of that case,' he said to his men. 'And to no more like it.'

'Hear, hear,' Peacock said.

They had all had more than enough of murder.

ACKNOWLEDGEMENTS

Thanks to Eileen, Andy, and Eve for their praise and comments. Plus, everyone I met on the Scottish Society of Authors writing retreat at Abbotsford, Sir Walter Scott's country home, where I was finishing this off; in particular Margaret Skea who organized it – the ambience and company were definitely inspirational.

If you enjoyed this book, please let others know by leaving a quick review on Amazon. Also, if you spot anything untoward in the paperback, get in touch. We strive for the best quality and appreciate reader feedback.

editor@thebookfolks.com

www.thebookfolks.com

When a parlour maid finds her wealthy mistress dead, Detective Blades is called in to investigate. The lady of the house's lifestyle has changed considerably following the death of her father, so the police focus on her many apparent suitors. Which of them could have wanted her dead?

Available on Kindle and in paperback from Amazon.

A woman is killed near the beach. There is little evidence. But the crime bears the hallmarks of several similar murders some time ago. The trouble is that the man supposedly responsible was sent to the gallows...

Available on Kindle and in paperback from Amazon.

www.ingramcontent.com/pod-product-compliance
Lightning Source LLC
Chambersburg PA
CBHW032220190726
48289CB00007BA/2321